BEAVER RETURNS

Beaver and Wally Cleaver, those lovable TV characters, are once again involved in some of the most mad-cap adventures of their young lives. As usual, Beaver's impulsive, friendly nature leads him into one scrape after another. The older by five years, Wally is kept busy pulling his brother out of trouble. But just as soon as Wally has rescued Beaver from one tough spot, Beaver is found in still another one. Since most of the situations arise out of Beaver's wish to be helpful to Wally, the older boy can't be too hard on him. Wally does finally beg him, though, "Please, Beaver, don't try to *help* me!"

BEAVER AND WALLY

Beverly Cleary

**Based on the television series
created by Joe Connelly
and Bob Mosher**

WILDSIDE PRESS

CONTENTS

BEAVER GOES TO THE CARNIVAL

Beaver Cleaver, whose real name was Theodore, was pretty much like any other fifth-grade boy in the town of Mayfield. He lived in a tree-shaded house on a winding street, he ate peanut-butter sandwiches after school and he rarely combed his hair unless his mother or father reminded him.

But there was one way in which Beaver was different

from any other boy in Mayfield School. Beaver was the only one who had Wally Cleaver for a brother. All the girls admired Wally's good looks and all the boys admired his letterman's sweater. Wally was not only on the high school basketball and swimming teams, he was a star on the track team. Everybody in Miss Landers' room thought Beaver was lucky to have Wally for a brother, and Beaver did too. Wally was something to brag about.

Lately Wally's behavior had puzzled Beaver. When his friend Eddie Haskell telephoned him, Wally no longer talked so the rest of the family could hear. Now he said, "Hi, Eddie, just a minute till I close the doors," and when all the doors were closed he talked in such a low voice Beaver could not hear a word he was saying, not even when he pressed his ear against the door. Naturally Beaver was curious to know why Wally had become so mysterious all of a sudden.

There was something else puzzling about Wally's behavior, something that worried Beaver. Although his father paid him a fair allowance, Wally was suddenly eager to earn money. He had even baby-sat with Chuckie, one of the little boys in the neighborhood. It was all right to earn money, but Beaver thought this was going too far—everyone knew baby-sitting was girl's work. Beaver could not help wondering if Wally was in some kind of trouble.

He wondered if Wally had broken somebody's picture window playing ball, but he doubted if this could happen. Wally was too good at both pitching and catching. Then he wondered if Eddie Haskell had got him into some kind of trouble. That could be. Eddie was the kind of boy who was full of schemes that could lead to trouble—usually for other people.

Beaver was still trying to figure out what Wally was up to when one Saturday his brother came home late for lunch. Mrs. Cleaver had decided not to wait for him and Beaver and his father had just sat down at the table in the kitchen when Wally came bursting through the back door. He was obviously excited about something. He was also very dirty.

"Hey, Dad, guess what!" Wally exclaimed. "I've got a job!"

"Wally, you smell like a stable." Mrs. Cleaver wrinkled her nose.

"Where is this job?" asked Mr. Cleaver. "In a stable?"

"It's at the carnival, Dad," Wally went on, "and the man is going to give me ten whole dollars at the end of the day!"

"You mean they pay you real money for working at at the carnival?" asked Beaver, who would have been glad to work for nothing because the carnival, which had been in Mayfield for the past week, was such an interesting place.

"Gee, Dad, it's neat," said Wally. "I get to carry water and sweep up and rub down horses and help the man clean the animals' cages." Then he added hastily, with a glance in his mother's direction, "Not when the animals are in them, though."

"Wally, you can't come to the table smelling like that," said Mrs. Cleaver. "You run along upstairs and take a bath."

"But Mom," protested Wally, "I don't have time. I have to get back to work."

"Can I come?" asked Beaver, pleased that Wally was earning money working for a carnival instead of baby-sitting. Beaver was ashamed to have Wally baby-sit and had hoped no one at school would find out about it.

"I can't stop you from coming to the carnival, but don't hang around me," said Wally. "I got work to do."

Mrs. Cleaver handed Wally a sandwich on a plate. "You eat this on the back steps," she said. "You aren't clean enough to come to the table."

Wally took the sandwich but not the plate. "If you don't mind, Mom, I'll just eat this on the way back to the carnival. That way I'll save time."

Mrs. Cleaver smiled in a half-amused, half-annoyed way, "All right, Wally, but you have to come home in time for a bath before dinner. Not just a shower but a good long soak in the tub."

"Sure, Mom," agreed Wally. "I'll get cleaned up. This is the night I go to the cook-out in Mary Ellen Rogers' backyard. Remember?" And with that he was gone.

This was another thing about Wally that had bothered Beaver lately. If he knew he was going to see a girl, especially Mary Ellen Rogers, he did not in the least mind getting cleaned up. He even rubbed lilac-smelling stuff in his curly brown hair. "Gee, ten whole dollars for doing something that's fun," said Beaver dreamily. "Do you suppose the carnival would give me a job, too? I could sweep and clean out the animals' cages, too. I know I could. I've helped clean out the garage lots of times."

"I'm afraid not, Beaver," said his father. "You are a little young. Besides, Wally doesn't have the ten dollars yet. When I was a boy, carnivals were known to skip town without paying their bills." Mr. Cleaver was inclined to reminisce about his own boyhood. Things were almost always harder when he was a boy. Snow was deeper, allowances smaller, fathers stricter.

"Ward, I don't like the idea of Wally working around that carnival. He might get hurt, and he's sure to meet some pretty rough people," said Mrs. Cleaver. "And if there is a chance he might really not get paid, why did you let him do it?"

"What kind of rough people, Mom?" asked Beaver, who thought that an opportunity to meet rough people made Wally's job more attractive.

"Oh . . . just rough people," answered Mrs. Cleaver vaguely.

Mr. Cleaver smiled the way he did when he was thinking of something that happened a long time ago. "Rubbing down horses, cleaning cages, carrying water— I didn't think there was anything that wonderful left in the world for kids to do."

Beaver understood exactly what his father meant and he could not wait to go to the carnival, if not to work himself, at least to watch his brother work. He gulped down his lunch, said good-bye to his parents and was on his way.

The carnival, which was set up on some vacant land at the edge of town by the railroad track, was noisy and dusty. Barkers shouted to attract customers to the side-shows, the Ferris wheel creaked, the merry-go-round blared. "Peanuts, popcorn, crackerjacks! Only twenty cents, the fifth part of a dollar!" called out the vendors who wandered through the crowd with trays of wares. "Real live chameleons! Get your real live chameleons here!"

It seemed to Beaver that everyone in Mayfield was attending the carnival. He saw two girls from his class, Judy Hensler and Violet Rutherford, standing in front of a fortune teller's tent trying to get up courage to go inside. As usual they were giggling.

"There's Beaver," said Violet. "Hi, Beaver! Why don't you come and get your fortune told?"

"No, thanks," said Beaver coldly. He did not even want to be seen talking to such a silly pair. Especially not to that old freckle-faced Violet Rutherford. Naturally his answer sent the girls into a gale of giggles. Embarrassed by their behavior, Beaver walked on. He thought of several answers he could have given Violet, but he had orders from his father to be nice to Violet. Her father and Mr. Cleaver worked in the same office and the two families sometimes got together for picnics or dinners.

"I think that Beaver Cleaver is the most stuck-up boy in our room at school," he heard Violet say to Judy. "I can't stand him."

This did not hurt Beaver's feelings a bit, because he could not stand Violet either. He continued his tour of the carnival until he saw his friends Gilbert and Whitey feeding peanuts to the carnival's one elephant. "Hi!" he called. Naturally he would rather talk to boys than girls anytime.

"Hey, Beaver, let's go see if they've got a tattooed man," suggested Whitey.

"Nope," answered Beaver. "I've got to find my brother Wally. He's got a job here."

"You mean Wally is really working for the carnival?" asked Gilbert.

"Sure. He's getting paid ten dollars." Beaver tried not to sound as if he were bragging. Continuing his search for Wally, he saw Eddie Haskell and Mary Ellen Rogers standing in front of a cage that housed a dusty old lion. "Hey, Eddie, have you seen Wally?" Beaver asked. "He's working someplace around here."

"No, I haven't seen him," answered Eddie, pulling

a comb out of his pocket and running it through his wavy blond hair. "What's he working for? Doesn't your dad give him an allowance?"

It was remarks like this that kept Beaver from really liking Eddie. That and the way he was always combing that wavy hair of his. "He wants to, that's why," answered Beaver, and wondered once more if perhaps Eddie had managed to get Wally into some kind of trouble.

"Eddie Haskell, I think it's perfectly wonderful for Wally to get a job with the carnival," Mary Ellen Rogers said.

"What's he doing?" asked Eddie.

"Watering horses," answered Beaver. "Important things."

"My dad wouldn't want me to be a common laborer," boasted Eddie. "He would want me to use my head, not my hands. It pays better."

But it wouldn't be as much fun, thought Beaver, and went on searching for Wally.

Beaver stopped and bought some popcorn and lingered at a shooting gallery until someone won a kewpie doll. He ate some peanuts and drank some pink lemonade as he watched a group of people trying to guess their weights. When no one won a prize he moved on until he came to the merry-go-round. He started to buy a ticket and then changed his mind because he would not find Wally while riding around and around. When he still did not see Wally he decided to go for a ride on the Ferris wheel, hoping that when he got up in the air he might have a better view of the carnival.

As it turned out, Beaver did have a good view of the carnival and a long one. He climbed into the seat and hung onto the bar in front of him as the big wheel turned and he rose to the top. There he stuck, swinging gently back and forth, while some carnival workers tinkered with the machinery down below. He looked around at the scene below him and finally spotted Wally lugging a bucket of water to some horses tethered behind one of the tents. "Hey, Wally!" he yelled.

Wally set down the bucket, wiped his forehead on his sleeve, picked up the bucket and walked on. He had not heard Beaver above the noises of the carnival.

It seemed to Beaver that he spent half the afternoon up in the air waiting for the Ferris wheel to be repaired. When he finally reached the ground again he pushed his way through the crowd to Wally.

"Oh, hi." Wearily Wally set down the heavy bucket he was lugging. Once more he wiped his grimy, sweaty face on his sleeve. His shirt was soaked with sweat and the water that had sloshed from the bucket onto his shoes had mixed with the dust of the carnival grounds to make mud. He did not look as enthusiastic about his job as he had at lunchtime.

"Boy, are you a mess," said Beaver.

"Yeah," agreed Wally. It was easy to see how tired he was. He opened and closed his right hand. There was a row of blisters across the palm.

"Gee . . ." Beaver did not like to see Wally get blisters on his hand. "Why don't you quit?"

"I can't," said Wally. "They aren't going to pay me until five-thirty and I need that ten dollars."

"What for?" asked Beaver, feeling that a ten-dollar bill was not worth a row of blisters. "Dad gives you an allowance."

"Sure he does," agreed Wally. "But a fellow can always use extra money for things. You know."

Beaver did know. He was always glad to earn a little extra money doing chores around the house so he could see another movie or have a couple of sodas. Still, he was puzzled. He could not think of anything he wanted enough to get blisters for.

"Hey, you over there!" yelled one of the carnival workers. "Get to work!"

Wally picked up the bucket of water and lugged it over to the horses, while Beaver sat on a bale of hay to watch. His mother had been right. The regular carnival workers were a tough-looking bunch. Working for the carnival no longer seemed like fun. It was hard, dirty work and Beaver was glad he was only a spectator.

Late in the afternoon the crowd began to melt away. When the last horse had been watered, Wally flopped down on the bale of hay beside Beaver.

"Wow!" said Beaver. "If Mom thought you smelled like a stable at lunchtime, she ought to get a whiff of you now."

"Yeah," said Wally wearily. "I need that good long soak in the bathtub and I'll have to wash my hair about four times before I can go to Mary Ellen Rogers' cookout."

"You better get going," Beaver reminded him. "It's getting late."

"Wait here while I go collect my pay," said Wally.

Beaver sat on the bale of hay and chewed a straw for a long time until a mighty discouraged looking Wally returned.

"I can't seem to find the man," said Wally, dropping down on the bale of hay once more. "I've looked all around the trucks and every place."

"Maybe he skipped out," suggested Beaver. "Dad

says in the old days when he was a boy carnivals sometimes skipped out without paying their bills."

"Aw, things were different when Dad was a kid," said Wally. "You know how he is, always talking about how hard things used to be. This man can't skip out. He's got to load these horses tonight when the carnival moves on. I'll just have to wait here until he turns up."

"It's getting late and you've got to soak," Beaver reminded him. "Mom isn't going to like you smelling like that and tracking up the house."

"Yeah, and I've got to put something on these blisters." Wally examined his painful hand. "Hey, Beaver, I know what. You wait here and get the money for me while I go home and get cleaned up."

"Not me," said Beaver.

"Aw, come on, Beav," pleaded Wally.

Beaver thought about Wally's blisters and began to relent. Blisters could be serious. "How do I know who the man is and if he really is going to pay you?" he asked suspiciously, afraid there might be some truth in what his father had said.

"His name is Willie and he's got the American flag tattooed on one arm and 'Mother' on the other," said Wally. "A guy like that couldn't be a crook."

"O.K.," said Beaver dubiously. "You go home and start soaking and I'll sit here until this Willie shows up."

Beaver did not have to wait long for Willie. As soon as Wally had gone, a man with the American flag tattooed on one arm and "Mother" on the other appeared from behind a tent. There was no mistaking Willie. He was a large man who had once had a broken nose. Twice, maybe. Beaver could see that Willie was one of the rough characters his mother had worried about.

"Hello," said Beaver bravely. "My brother had to go home and I've stayed to collect the ten dollars you owe him."

"Get lost, kid," said Willie.

"I will not!" said Beaver indignantly, thinking of those painful blisters on Wally's hand. "You owe my brother ten dollars."

Willie spat into the dust. "Yeah? How do I know you really are his brother?"

This stopped Beaver. "I—I just am, is all."

Willie started to lead a horse up a ramp into a truck.

Beaver did not think it was time to load the horses, because the carnival would not break up until late that evening, but he could be mistaken. Perhaps Willie had to travel on ahead with the horses. If Beaver let him get away, Wally would never get his ten dollars. "You— you pay me my brother's ten dollars or I'll tell the police," he said, feeling this was the only way to deal with a rough character. "That's what I'll do."

"Now don't get huffy." Willy sounded almost kind. "I didn't say I wasn't going to pay you the ten dollars, did I? You and me can be friends. Want to see me wave my flag?" Willie doubled up his fist and began to flex his muscles so that the flag tattooed on his arm began to ripple.

Beaver tried to ignore this fascinating sight. "No, we can't be friends," he said stoutly. "Not until I get the ten dollars. And now I'm going to go tell the police." He turned as if he were about to leave, even though he had no idea where he could find a policeman.

Willie walked down the ramp from the truck, spat once more into the dust and said, "Tell you what I'll do, kid. I'll give you something better than ten dollars."

"What?" asked Beaver suspiciously. Willie had better not try to put anything over on *him*.

"I'll give you a horse," said Willie.

"A—a whole horse?" asked Beaver in astonishment.

Willie grinned. "Sure. You didn't think I'd give you half a horse, did you?"

"Well . . . no." Beaver was still astonished. "You mean a real honest-to-goodness live horse?" The thought crossed Beaver's mind that this might be some kind of grownup joke. Perhaps if he agreed to accept a horse instead of ten dollars Willie would hand him a hobby horse.

"Real live honest-to-goodness horse." Willie leaned against a fence post. "Now this here horse is a genuine circus horse worth more than ten dollars. His mother and father were Russian horses and his name is Nicholas. Nick to his friends, and I can tell you and Nick are going to be great friends. On his back he has carried the most famous bareback riders in the history of the circus. And let me tell you something . . ." Willie leaned forward as if he were telling Beaver something very confidentially. "This here horse is worth more than a *hundred* dollars."

"Gee . . ." Beaver was beginning to be awed.

"He has performed before the crowned heads of Europe," continued Willie.

"Boy . . ." Now Beaver was really awed.

"Real kings and queens," said Willie.

Beaver did not know what to say.

"Well, take it or leave it, kid," said Willie briskly. "I got work to do."

"I—I guess I'll take it," said Beaver, bewildered by

the unexpected offer. A real circus horse that had performed before the crowned heads of Europe! Of course he would take it. Why, Wally would be the only boy in Mayfield to have a real live circus horse, and maybe he would even let Beaver be half owner because he had been lucky enough to get it. "Which horse is it?"

Willie led forth a white horse. It was no larger than any other circus horse, but to Beaver it looked enormous. "The biggest animal I ever had was a rabbit," said Beaver, looking up at Nick.

"And to show you my heart is in the right place, I'll even throw in the blanket absolutely free of charge." Willie pulled a blanket off the fence and laid it across Nick's back.

"Gee . . ." Beaver still could not believe his luck. A real horse! He could hardly wait to see how pleased Wally was going to be. He took the rope that Willie handed him. "Thanks, mister. Thanks a lot."

"I told you me and you could be friends," Willie reminded him.

"You sure did," said Beaver, thinking that he had been pretty smart not to let Willie get the better of him. This would show his father that carnivals weren't like they used to be.

Beaver started for home with Nicholas clopping obediently along behind him. He felt pretty important to be leading the only genuine circus horse in all of Mayfield, and he was pleased when people turned to stare at him. Wait until the kids at school saw him riding around on a horse that had performed before the crowned heads of Europe! They would all be begging him for rides. He might let Whitey and Gilbert have a ride, but Judy and Violet—never! No matter how hard they begged him he would not let them ride Nick. They could pat him on the neck, but that was all.

Nick nickered softly as he clopped along behind Beaver. "Good old Nick," answered Beaver. It was nice to have a horse to talk to.

But as Beaver began to approach his house he walked more and more slowly. There were certain practical problems attached to keeping a horse that had not occurred to him until now. His father just might not be as pleased as Wally. Naturally the Cleavers did not have a stable. Nick would have to sleep in the garage and Beaver was not at all certain his father would want to leave his car in the driveway every night. And then there was the problem of food for Nick. He could eat the grass in the yard, but where would he get any hay and oats? Those cost money and Wally wasn't going to want to spend any money on Nick until he had figured out a way to earn money with a horse.

And Wally would want to use Nick to earn money. The way he had been acting lately, Beaver was sure of that. Well, Wally was good at figuring things out. He would know what to say to his father about Nick.

Fortunately no one was looking out the window when Beaver and Nick reached home. Beaver led the horse on the grass beside the driveway so his hoofs would not make any noise on the concrete. He led him quietly into the garage and tied him to the workbench, where he hoped the horse might not be noticed until he had a chance to explain the situation to Wally. "Now you be quiet," he said, and patted the animal on the neck.

Then it occurred to Beaver that Wally had probably already left for Mary Ellen Rogers' cook-out and he might have to explain Nick to his father himself. He went into the house wondering how he was going to bring a horse into the conversation. Somehow he did not think he could just blurt out, "Say, Dad, I have a horse in the garage."

THE HORSE NAMED NICK

When Beaver slipped quietly into the house he found that Wally had indeed already left for Mary Ellen Rogers' house. As he washed his hands and tried to slick down his hair he decided it was wisest not to mention Nick to his father until he had to. Beaver ate his supper in silence because his thoughts were occupied with Nick tied to the workbench out there in the garage.

He wondered if Nick was hungry. He was pretty sure he could not be thirsty—not after all the water Wally had carried that afternoon.

"Well, Beaver," said Mr. Cleaver, "for a boy who spent the afternoon at a carnival you don't have much to say. Wally tells me he left you to collect his money for him. Did the man pay you or did he skip out without paying, the way carnival people did when I was a boy?"

"Oh, he paid all right," said Beaver, and to change the subject he went on quickly. "I went for a ride on the Ferris wheel and got stuck up at the top. I had to sit there a long time but I had a keen view of the whole carnival."

From the garage came the faint sound of a whinny. Beaver wondered uneasily if Nick was asking for his supper and how much noise he would make if he did not get it right away.

"That's funny," remarked Mrs. Cleaver. "I thought I heard a horse."

"Don't be silly, dear," said Mr. Cleaver. "There aren't any horses around here."

"Practically everybody in Mayfield was at the carnival," said Beaver hastily. "There was a real big crowd and—"

The telephone cut him short. Mrs. Cleaver went into the living room to answer it and Beaver could hear her voice coming through the hall. "Oh yes. What? Are you sure? Oh, I see. Yes, well, thank you very much. We certainly appreciate it." She returned to the dining room looking a little dazed.

"Who was that?" asked Mr. Cleaver.

"It was Chuckie's mother from across the street,"

answered Mrs. Cleaver, still looking dazed. "She says there is a horse in our garage."

Mr. Cleaver laughed. "A horse in our garage! She must be seeing things."

Mrs. Cleaver looked worried. "I don't know . . . she was so insistent."

"Now, June," said Mr. Cleaver, "be reasonable. How would a horse get into our garage? There's no horse there. Now let's finish our dinner."

From the garage came the faint sound of Nick's whinny.

Mrs. Cleaver laid her napkin by her plate and started to rise from the table. "I *know* I heard a horse," she said.

"Sit down, dear," said Mr. Cleaver, sounding a little impatient. "You're imagining things."

"But Dad," said Beaver in a small voice, "there *is* a horse in the garage." His father had to know sometime. It might as well be now.

Mr. Cleaver laid his fork down and looked at his son. "Did I hear you say there is a horse in our garage?"

Beaver looked down at his plate. "Yes, Dad."

"And how, may I ask, did this horse get in our garage?" Mr. Cleaver wanted to know.

"Well . . . uh . . . I led him there," confessed Beaver. "I . . . uh . . . didn't know where else to put him so I tied him to the workbench."

"Beaver!" exclaimed Mrs. Cleaver. "What on earth are you talking about?"

Mr. Cleaver threw down his napkin. "Come on. Let's go out and have a look at this horse."

Reluctantly Beaver followed his mother and father to the garage. He hoped that somehow Nick would have disappeared, but there he was, still tied to the

workbench, and looking, it seemed to Beaver, very sad,
for a horse.

"All right, Beaver," said Mr. Cleaver. "Start explain-
ing."

Beaver gulped. "Well, you see, Dad . . . well, it was
like this. Wally had to come home to get cleaned up
so he asked me to find the man named Willie and get
the money from him. And Willie said he would give
me something better than ten dollars. He would give
me a real Russian circus horse." Beaver glanced at his
father, who looked stern. "The man . . . said he was
worth . . . over a hundred dollars," Beaver finished
falteringly. "His name is Nicholas. Nick for short."

"I don't think Wally is going to like this," said Mrs.
Cleaver.

Beaver was sure his mother was wrong. Wally would
know a bargain when he saw one.

"There isn't any question about it," said Mr. Cleaver.
"You can't accept a horse. Come on, let's get in the
car and we'll go find this Willie, get Wally's money,
and have Willie come and get his horse."

Maybe this was the best way out. Beaver was glad
to climb into the car beside his father and ride to the
carnival grounds. If they collected the ten dollars and
returned the horse, maybe Wally would not have to
know about Nick at all. Beaver did not want Wally to
be disappointed over having a ten-dollar bill instead of
a hundred-dollar horse.

When the Cleavers reached the carnival grounds
they could not find Willie. They asked around all the
tents and animal cages but no one seemed to know anything about a man named Willie. They did not even
know about a man with the American flag tattooed on
one arm and "Mother" on the other.

"Willie? Never heard of him," one carnival worker would say and then call out to someone else, "Hey, Joe! Know anything about a guy named Willie?"

"Never heard of him," Joe would answer. "Been with the carnival two years and never heard of no one called Willie. Must be some other carnival you're thinking of."

"Something tells me we're getting the runaround," said Mr. Cleaver.

"And something tells me we still have a horse at home in the garage," said Mrs. Cleaver.

"I guess I better pull some grass for Nick's supper," said Beaver.

That night Beaver was in bed asleep when Wally came home. The next morning, when he woke up, Wally was sleeping soundly with his bandaged hand resting on his pillow. Beaver dressed quietly and slipped downstairs to breakfast without waking Wally. He had not finished eating when Wally, still looking sleepy, came down the stairs.

"Where did you put it, Beav?" asked Wally, and yawned.

"Put what?" asked Beaver, knowing very well what Wally meant but not knowing where to begin the story that now seemed pretty complicated.

"You did get it, didn't you?" demanded Wally suspiciously.

"Well . . . you see, Wally, it was like this," said Beaver. "I got a real Russian circus horse instead."

"A horse?" Wally was incredulous.

"Yes, and the man said it was worth at least a hundred dollars," said Beaver quickly. "And that's ten times ten dollars."

"I can multiply, too." Beaver had never seen his

brother look so disgusted. "Honest, Beaver, I just don't know . . ." He shook his head. "Jeepers, a horse! What am I supposed to do with a horse? It's money I need."

"Well, golly, Wally . . ." Beaver's feelings were hurt by his brother's reaction. "It's a real circus horse. It has performed before the crowned heads of Europe."

"Ahh—the crowned heads of Europe!" Wally's disgust increased.

"Nick isn't just any old horse," said Beaver defensively. "And the man threw in his blanket absolutely free."

"Now boys," said Mr. Cleaver, "suppose we go out to the garage and have a look at Nick and see what we can do about the situation."

"A horse," muttered Wally. "For Pete's sake, a horse."

"Gee, Wally," said Beaver, on the way out the back door, "if that's the way you feel about it, I'll give you my allowance every week until you have your ten dollars. I would like to have a horse."

"It's not that simple, Beaver," said Mr. Cleaver. "Where would you ride him?"

"Gee, Dad, I don't have to ride him anyplace. I can just come out here in the garage and sit on him. And he can eat the grass in the backyard. That way you wouldn't have to mow it all the time."

"I don't want to wait a million years for my ten dollars," said Wally. "I need it now."

Mr. Cleaver opened the garage door. There was Nick stretched out on the floor with his eyes closed.

Beaver was horrified. "Dad, what's wrong with him?"

"He's dead," said Wally angrily. "That's what's the matter with him."

As if in answer, Nick opened his eyes. He looked very, very sad.

"He isn't either dead," said Beaver indignantly, now that he was sure the horse was still alive. "He must have had a dizy spell and fainted." He knelt and patted Nick's head. "What do you think is wrong with him, Dad?"

Mrs. Cleaver laid her hand on Nick's head the way she always laid her hand on Beaver's forehead when she thought he was coming down with a cold. "He doesn't seem to have a fever."

"I don't think that's the way you tell," said Mr. Cleaver, "but some horses do sleep lying down." He grasped Nick's halter. "Up, boy! Come on, boy. Up!"

"Too bad the crowned heads of Europe can't see him now," said Wally sarcastically.

Nick raised his head, looked wearily around, and laid it down again.

Wally groaned. "If he isn't dead, he's dying. There goes my ten bucks."

"Now wait," said Mr. Cleaver. "I'll look in the phone book and see if we can get a veterinarian to come over. In the meantime, let's leave the garage doors open. The air might do him some good."

"I'll go make another pot of coffee," said Mrs. Cleaver.

"Gee, Mom—for the horse?" asked Beaver.

"No, for us," answered his mother.

The veterinarian, who had a small animal hospital, did not treat horses. He suggested calling the agricultural college. Mr. Cleaver telephoned the college, which was in another town. They said they would treat the horse if Mr. Cleaver would load him in a trailer and bring him to the college. No one knew where to find a horse trailer on Sunday or how to get the horse to his feet and into the trailer even if they did find one.

"You know," said Wally, "maybe he's hungry."

"I think you've got something there, Wally," said Mr. Cleaver. And so the family drove out to a farm in the country to buy some oats and hay for Nick. Neither Beaver nor Wally said anything when Mr. Cleaver paid for the food. Beaver did not see why he should pay to feed Wally's horse and Wally, he knew, did not have any money or he would not be so eager to earn some.

At the sight of food Nicholas did rise stiffly to his feet to eat. Mr. Cleaver patted his neck and spoke soothingly to him. "Poor old fellow. He's had a hard life in that carnival."

"Ward, I don't think you should make Nick feel so much at home," said Mrs. Cleaver. "You know we're going to have to get rid of him."

"You can't just take a full-grown horse out and lose him," Mr. Cleaver pointed out. "There's probably a law against it."

"I'll say you can't take him out and lose him," said Wally. "He's my horse and we've got to figure out a way to get my money out of him. Maybe we can find somebody to buy him."

"Maybe we could rent him out for kids to ride," suggested Beaver, who was fond of Nick and did not want to see him sold.

"Hey, maybe we could, if we can keep him on his feet," agreed Wally hopefully. "I sure need the money."

With a great sigh Nick lay down on the garage floor once more and closed his eyes as if he were very, very tired.

"That settles that," said Wally in disgust. "Nobody is going to rent a horse that just lies around all day."

"Gee, Wally, I'm sorry," said Beaver truthfully. "I thought you'd be glad to have a horse worth a hundred dollars."

"Aw, well, I shouldn't have trusted you," said Wally. "You're just a kid. You didn't know any better."

This stung Beaver more than anything Wally could have said. No boy wants to be told he doesn't know any better, especially by his older brother. He would rather have Wally be good and mad at him, even yell at him and threaten to punch him in the nose, than this. Wally and Beaver did not say much to one another after that. Wally did not seem angry so much as gloomy, and that made Beaver feel worse than ever. He did not like being Wally's dumb kid brother.

Once Nick whinnied and the boys rushed hopefully out to the garage, only to find him still lying on the floor looking tired and sad. "Poor old Nick," said Beaver sorrowfully as he patted the horse on the neck.

It seemed to Beaver that he could think of nothing but Nick. He spent most of the day sitting beside him stroking his neck. He gathered some nice green grass and offered it to Nick, who nickered as if he might be grateful but did not eat it. Late in the afternoon Beaver went into the house to find some sugar cubes to tempt Nick. While he was hunting through the kitchen cupboard, he heard the front door chimes ring.

"Good afternoon," Mr. Cleaver said to someone when he opened the door.

Beaver went into the dining room to see who had come to call. It was a strange man in a uniform who was handing Mr. Cleaver a card.

"You're from the Board of Health?" said Mr. Cleaver, sounding surprised. "On Sunday?"

"Yep, this is an emergency," the man answered brusquely. "Where is it?"

By now Wally was looking over the banister railing to see what was going on.

"Where is what?" asked Mr. Cleaver.

"The dead horse," answered the man.

Mr. Cleaver smiled. "Well, I'm sorry to disappoint you, but we don't have a dead horse."

"The neighbors reported you did," the man informed him.

"That was a misunderstanding," said Mr. Cleaver. "The horse isn't dead. He was just . . . resting."

"Yes, he's very much alive," said Mrs. Cleaver, joining in the conversation.

Beaver did not think it was quite true to say that Nick was very much alive. Just barely alive would sound more like the truth.

"You got a live horse right here on the premises?" asked the man.

"Well, not right here," said Mr. Cleaver. "Out in the garage."

"Look, people, you can't stable a horse here in a residential neighborhood." The man looked stern.

"We're trying to find some way to get rid of him," answered Mr. Cleaver pleasantly.

"Mister, you're wide open for a violation," the man informed him.

"As long as you're here, maybe you could take him," suggested Mrs. Cleaver.

"Sorry, ma'am. I can't touch 'em unless they're dead." The man tipped his cap and started down the steps.

"Well, thank you anyway," said Mr. Cleaver, and

closed the door. Then he turned to his wife. "You know, dear, I imagine the fine is a rather large one."

"Gee, Dad, the only thing we can do is sell him," said Wally from the stairway. "At least I might get my money back."

"You boys can try," agreed Mr. Cleaver, "but I don't imagine there's much of a market for a tired old horse who likes to loll around the house all day."

"He'll be all right as soon as he gets rested up from that carnival," said Beaver loyally, but in his heart he was not so sure. Nick was the droopiest horse he had ever seen, and Beaver had begun to suspect that the droop was permanent.

Beaver followed Wally upstairs to the bedroom where Wally sat down at his desk, chewed thoughtfully on a pencil and then wrote something on a piece of paper. "O.K., Beaver, listen to this," he said, and began to read. " 'Genuine circus horse for sale. Intelligent, does not eat much. Very cheap, blanket included. Can do tricks like playing dead.' Then I'll stick our address in here."

"Sounds good to me," said Beaver. "You can put it in the paper under 'Used Horses' and probably some millionaire will buy him for his daughter and she'll stick him in a horse show and Nick will get his picture in the paper and be famous."

"You're goofy, Beaver," said Wally, with the first smile he had shown all day. "But at least somebody ought to buy him. I'll ask Mom to phone the ad to the paper the first thing in the morning. A live horse ought to be worth at least twenty dollars, don't you think?"

"Sure," agreed Beaver, who was eager to see Wally get the money he had worked so hard to earn. At the same time he was going to miss Nick, and he said so. "This afternoon he put his head right on my lap. I never had anything that big like me before."

"Yeah . . . I know," said Wally, "but you know how it is, Beaver. I worked to earn money, not a horse. And anyway, the city won't let us keep him. This ad has got to work or we're in trouble. Dad can joke about paying a fine to the city, but if he really got arrested and had to pay it he would just about raise the roof around here."

The next evening, as soon as the paper came, the boys searched for and found the advertisement in the "Pets for Sale" column. They agreed that someone should answer an advertisement for a horse that was such a bargain. They waited all evening for someone to come to look at Nick but no one came. Wally began to look discouraged. "Maybe people who buy horses want to look at them in the daytime," he suggested, but he did not look very hopeful.

The next day, however, when the boys came home from school they saw a truck and horse trailer parked in front of the house. "Hey, look!" yelled Beaver. "A customer for Nick!" The boys both began to run and ran straight to the garage, where they found a man looking at Nick. Fortunately Nick happened to be standing on his feet.

"Hello," said Wally. "Uh . . . are you interested in my horse?"

"Yes. My name is Johnson," answered the man. "Are you sure it's O.K. with your parents if you sell the horse?"

"Oh, sure," said Wally. "It's my horse and they said I could sell him."

Could sell him, thought Beaver. *Had* to sell him or

get arrested. "He's very gentle and he doesn't eat much," he said in an effort at salesmanship.

Mr. Johnson ran his hand over Nick's flank. "I'll give you twenty-five dollars for him."

"Why . . . sure," agreed Wally, and Beaver could tell he was trying not to sound too pleased because Mr. Johnson had offered more than he expected to get. "Twenty-five dollars seems like a fair price."

Mr. Johnson pulled out his wallet and counted out the money to Wally. "Ten . . . twenty . . . five. There you are." He untied Nick and started to lead him out of the garage, while Beaver and Wally exchanged a triumphant grin.

Twenty-five whole dollars, thought Beaver. That would show Wally he could be trusted.

"Hey, Mr. Johnson," Wally called. "Don't you want his blanket? It goes with him for free."

"No, son, I won't be needing that," answered Mr. Johnson.

"Good-bye, Nick," said Beaver. "And Mr. Johnson, if he lies down on the way home, he's not dead. He's only fooling." He was sorry to see Nick leave and followed him out to the trailer. "You going to put Nicholas in a horse show?" he asked.

Mr. Johnson smiled. "Well, not exactly, son. I have a rendering plant."

"Oh," Beaver watched Mr. Johnson coax Nick into the horse trailer. "Wally, what's a rendering plant?"

"I don't know exactly," answered Wally. "I think it's a place where they take old bones and junk and make it into glue and stuff and—" He stopped and stared at the horse trailer as if he had just had a terrible thought. Mr. Johnson climbed in the truck and started the motor.

"Hey, mister!" yelled Wally. "Mister, give us the horse back!" He ran up to the window of the truck.

"Yeah!" yelled Beaver, who suddenly understood why Wally was so upset. "You give us our horse back!"

Mr. Johnson leaned out the window. "Boys, we made a deal," he reminded them.

"Yes, but we didn't know you were going to make glue out of Nick," said Beaver.

"Now wait a minute, kids," Mr. Johnson began. "I paid you twenty-five dollars—"

"No, sir." Wally was emphatic as he held out the twenty-five dollars. "Here's your money back."

"O.K., O.K." Mr. Johnson turned off the motor, climbed out of the truck and backed Nick out of the trailer.

"I'm sorry," apologized Wally, "but—"

"That's O.K.," interrupted Mr. Johnson. "I know how it is. I always hate to take some kid's pet."

"That was close," remarked Beaver, as the boys led Nick back to the garage, where he sank once more to the floor with a weary sigh. Beaver was grateful to Wally for wanting to save poor old Nick. After all, twenty-five dollars was a lot of money.

"It sure was close," agreed Wally. "But now we're still stuck with the horse. If we don't get rid of him fast the neighbors will really kick up a fuss and Dad will have to pay that fine. He might even take it out of our allowances and if the fine turned out to be a couple of hundred dollars we wouldn't have any spending money for years."

"Maybe someone else will answer the ad," suggested Beaver, but he did not have much hope. He had sadly concluded that only a glue factory would want Nick.

"Gee, if we had sold Nick to that man, I wouldn't have used glue again for the rest of my life. Every time I licked a stamp, I'd've thought of Nick."

"Yeah," agreed Wally, "but I sort of dread Dad's asking if we got rid of him."

When Mr. Cleaver came home he parked the car in the driveway because Nick was still resting in the garage. "Well, boys, did you have any offers for Nick?" he asked when he came in the house.

"Just one," said Wally cautiously, "but the man went away."

Beaver could not help thinking that for a man who might have to pay a fine for keeping a horse in a residential neighborhood his father looked pretty cheerful.

"I did a little telephoning today," said Mr. Cleaver, "and I think our problem is solved."

"How, Dad?" Wally asked eagerly.

"I found somebody to take Nick," said Mr. Cleaver.

"Not a glue man?" Beaver was now suspicious of anyone who wanted a horse.

"No, nothing like that," Mr. Cleaver reassured him. "I called the man who sold us the hay and oats for Nick. He has agreed to take Nick."

"Hey, that's neat," said Beaver, relieved at this solution. Nick would probably be happier in the country than he was shut up in the garage. He might stand up more. "But I hope Nick won't have to work too hard. He's pretty old."

"I wouldn't worry about that, Beaver," said Mr. Cleaver. "Nick has worked all his life. He'll be happier if he's useful."

"And if he gets tired of working he's smart enough

to lie down," reassured Wally. 'And you know how hard it is to get him up once he's down."

"Yeah, I know." Beaver could laugh now that the problem of Nick was solved and his father would not be raising the roof about paying a fine to the city.

"Boy, that's a load off my mind," said Wally. "Now I will get my money out of Nick?"

Mr. Cleaver looked surprised. "Oh?"

"Well, sure, Dad," said Wally. "How much is the man paying for Nick?"

Mr. Cleaver rubbed his chin and looked embarrassed. "Well, Wally, it didn't exactly work out that way."

Now Wally was worried. "What do you mean, Dad?"

"The man isn't buying Nick," explained Mr. Cleaver. "He is going to give him a good home."

"You mean you let him have Nick free?" demanded Wally.

"Well, now let's face it, Wally," said Mr. Cleaver. "We couldn't keep the horse and we don't have any other way to get rid of it."

"I know," agreed Wally, "but I worked hard at that carnival and I could sure use the money."

Mr. Cleaver laid his hand on Wally's shoulder. "Cheer up, Wally. I'll pay the twenty dollars it's going to cost to get Nick hauled to the farm. It won't cost you and Beaver a cent."

Wally groaned. "Twenty bucks!"

"Gee, Wally, it could be worse," Beaver reminded his brother. "Dad could take the twenty dollars out of our allowances."

"Yeah, I know," said Wally.

Beaver looked curiously at his brother. "Dad gives you a fair allowance. How come you're so keen on earning money all of a sudden?"

To Beaver's surprise Wally looked embarrassed. "Aw, none of your business," he muttered, and gave Beaver a playful punch on the arm.

CHUCKIE'S NEW SHOES

One Saturday morning not long after Nick had been sent to the country, Mr. and Mrs. Cleaver were going out to do some errands. At the door Mrs. Cleaver turned and said to her sons, "We may not be back till after lunch, so don't you boys get in any trouble."

"Gee, I'm in the fifth grade and Wally's in high

school," Beaver reminded his mother. "What kind of trouble could we get into?"

Mr. Cleaver smiled at the boys as he pulled his car keys out of his pocket. "Well, if you boys can't think of any trouble to get into, I would say you're not very imaginative."

Beaver laughed. "Hey, that's pretty funny, Dad."

"I don't think he meant it to be funny, Beav," explained Wally. "I think it's a kind of hint that we shouldn't goof around. Don't worry about me, Dad. I've got a job this morning."

"Oh? What's that, Wally?" Mr. Cleaver wanted to know.

"Nothing much," said Wally. "I'm going to take Chuckie Murdock downtown to get some new shoes. His mother can't do it because she has to stay home with the new baby."

"That's nice, Wally," said Mrs. Cleaver. "I'm glad you can help her out."

Beaver was not glad. He did not even like to have Wally go across the street to baby-sit with Chuckie, and now he was planning to take him downtown so that everybody in Mayfield would know that Wally Cleaver, track star of Mayfield High, was a baby-sitter. Beaver did not see how Wally could bring himself to do such a thing.

"She's paying me a dollar to do it," said Wally.

"I'm glad you have a chance to earn some money," said Mr. Cleaver. "See you later, boys."

"Aw, what do you have to go and take Chuckie downtown for?" asked Beaver, when his parents had gone. "Now everybody in town will know you're a baby-sitter."

"I need the dollar," said Wally. "Anyway Chuckie

isn't exactly a baby and, like Mom said, it's nice to help Mrs. Murdock out."

Money again. "What do you need the money for?" Beaver asked curiously. "Dad gives you an allowance."

"Oh . . . stuff," said Wally vaguely. "You know how it is. A fellow can always use extra money."

Beaver did know how it was. He was always glad to earn a little extra money now and then himself, although he certainly would never go so far as to baby-sit. Right now he was saving up to buy a surplus weather balloon and was always glad to add to the fund. This did not make him any happier about having everyone in Mayfield and especially in Miss Landers' room at school see Wally baby-sitting in public.

Wally said, "Well, it's about time for Mrs. Murdock to bring Chuckie over. She didn't want me ringing the doorbell and waking up the baby." He was about to open the door when the chimes rang.

Instead of Mrs. Murdock and Chuckie, it was Eddie Haskell with a pair of ice skates slung over his shoulder. "Don't just stand there," he said to Wally. "Let's go."

"Let's go where?" Wally wanted to know.

"What do you mean where?" asked Eddie. "That new ice-skating rink opens today. You said you'd go with me."

"I know, Eddie," admitted Wally, "but I've sort of got to do an errand for a neighbor lady. I'm going to take her little boy downtown to buy some shoes."

Eddie laughed. "Come on, Wally, who do you think you are? Captain Kangaroo?"

"Gee, Eddie, I promised, and besides I need the money," said Wally. "Here comes Mrs. Murdock with Chuckie now."

Mrs. Murdock was plainly in a hurry. She handed

the six-year-old boy in a green sweater over to Wally and said, "Now remember, get the same kind of shoes he has on, only in a larger size. I have already telephoned the store and told them a boy is bringing Chuckie in for his shoes and that it's perfectly all right for him to charge them to my account."

"Oh, sure," said Wally, taking Chuckie by the hand.

"Bye-bye, Chuckie. Be a good boy," said Mrs. Murdock, and hurried back across the street.

"Wally, you can't let me down," said Eddie. "I promised Mary Ellen Rogers and all the girls I was bringing you. If I show up by myself, they won't even talk to me."

"But I'm stuck." Wally looked unhappy. "Besides, you know I need that dollar."

"Yeah," agreed Eddie.

"And I don't think I should spend money ice skating," added Wally. "I need it for other things."

"Don't worry about that," said Eddie. "My dad gave me a couple of free passes. My dad knows all the important people in Mayfield."

Why does he need that dollar, Beaver wondered, and at the same time he had an idea. Maybe he could take Chuckie downtown in Wally's place. Nobody would ever suspect him of baby-sitting because once in a great while when there was no one his own age around Beaver sometimes played with Chuckie. People would just think he was walking down the street with a little boy he sometimes played with. It would be different with Wally, who was much older than Chuckie. As for buying the shoes—that would be easy. The store was already expecting a boy instead of Mrs. Murdock.

"I could do it," he told Wally. "I don't have anything else to do this morning."

"Yeah, but I've got to have that dollar," repeated Wally.

Beaver felt there were some things more important than money—things like not having the boys and girls in Miss Landers' room make fun of him because his brother baby-sat. "I'll do it for a dime," he offered. "That way you can keep ninety cents." This seemed fair enough. After all, it was Wally who got the job.

"You sure you're grown-up enough?" Wally sounded doubtful.

"Sure. I'm a monitor at school. I know how to push little kids around," boasted Beaver.

"Well, O.K.," agreed Wally. "Come on, Eddie. I think my skates are in the garage, and I want to get my sweater." Wally always wore his letterman's sweater when he knew he was going to see some girls.

Chuckie, who did not understand that Beaver played with him only when there was no one his own age to play with, was happy to start downtown with him. At first everything went smoothly. They passed Violet Rutherford, who merely said "Hi" and did not even giggle. Beaver said "Hi" right back and felt that he had fulfilled the minimum requirements of politeness required by his father toward all members of the Rutherford family. Beaver saw several other people he knew but no one seemed to think it unusual that he was walking along the street with Chuckie.

Then they came to an ice-cream truck. "Beaver, buy me an ice-cream bar," demanded Chuckie.

"I'm not supposed to buy you anything but shoes," Beaver told him.

"But I want an ice-cream bar," insisted Chuckie.

"No," said Beaver. "Come on, Chuckie."

"If you don't buy me an ice-cream bar, I'm going to yell," threatened Chuckie.

Beaver was not going to be intimidated. "Go ahead and yell," he said. "See if I care."

Chuckie did as he was told. He opened his mouth and let out a yell, a loud yell that could be heard for at least two blocks. It sounded as if he were scared, angry and hurt all at the same time. It was a good rousing yell. Beaver quickly put his hand over the little boy's mouth and said, "One ice-cream bar, please, mister." He could not have Chuckie going around making noises like that. He paid for the bar with a dime out of his own pocket, thereby losing his profit for the morning.

Eating the ice-cream bar and getting his face smeared with chocolate occupied Chuckie the rest of the way downtown. He was licking his sticky fingers when they reached the department store. Beaver led him to the shoe department and saw that he was seated on a chair, not on the shoe-clerk's stool.

"And what can I do for you, young men?" asked the clerk.

"Mrs. Murdock—that's Chuckie's mother—says to get him shoes like he has on, only bigger," explained Beaver.

"Oh, yes, Mrs. Murdock," said the clerk. "She telephoned to say you were coming in and that the shoes were to be charged to her account." He removed Chuckie's shoe and had him stand on the measuring stick. Then he found a pair of shoes and tried them on the little boy. "Stand up. How does that feel?" he asked.

"It feels fine," said Chuckie, not paying much attention to his shoes.

"Is it all right back here?" asked the clerk, as he squeezed Chuckie's heel.

"It feels fine," repeated Chuckie, looking around the shoe department.

"Now walk up and down," directed the clerk. "Does it hurt anywhere?"

"No, they feel fine."

"Shall I wrap them up?" the clerk asked Beaver.

"Yes, sir," said Beaver, glad buying shoes for Chuckie had turned out to be so easy.

"I don't like them," announced Chuckie in a loud, clear voice.

"Chuckie, you just said they were fine," protested Beaver. "Why don't you like them?"

"I want shoes with the toes out," Chuckie informed him. "When I'm walking I want to see what my toes are doing."

"You can't see what your toes are doing," said Beaver crossly. "You've got to take these. Your mother said so."

Chuckie pointed to some sandals. "If I don't get those I'm going to yell."

The clerk looked at Beaver and said in a low voice, as if they were sharing a secret, "Why don't we let him yell?"

Beaver sighed. He could not let Chuckie give his scared-angry-hurt yell right out loud in the middle of the department store. Beaver, who had been willing to bring Chuckie downtown, was not willing to attract that much attention. "I tried it once, mister. You wouldn't like it."

"Then what are we going to do?" asked the clerk.

Beaver thought it over while Chuckie's scowl grew darker by the second. "Well . . . Chuckie, if I get you the shoes with the no toes, will you take the shoes with the toes?"

"O.K., Beaver," said Chuckie, cheerfully and promptly.

The clerk found the proper sandals for Chuckie, tied the two shoe boxes together with a string and handed them to Beaver. "There you are," he said, as if he were glad the sale was completed. "Now would you step over to the desk and sign for them."

"I want to carry the shoes," announced Chuckie.

"No, I'll carry them," said Beaver, who wanted to be sure the shoes reached Mrs. Murdock.

"If you don't let me carry them, I'm going to—" began Chuckie.

"Here, you carry them," said Beaver hastily, and followed the clerk to the desk, where the clerk handed him the sales book to sign. This made Beaver feel very grown up. He had never signed for a charged purchase before. He wanted to be sure he did everything right, so he read the sales slip carefully. "What's this?" he asked, pointing to a figure. "We didn't buy anything for twenty-four cents."

"That is sales tax," explained the clerk.

"Oh, sure." Embarrassed that he had forgotten about the sales tax, Beaver signed the slip. When he turned around Chuckie was gone.

Beaver felt a moment of panic. "Where did he go?" he asked the clerk.

"Now don't worry," said the clerk. "He's around here someplace." He looked behind a display case and called, "Little boy! Little boy!" There was no little boy behind the display case.

"Chuckie!" called Beaver, looking behind the rows of chairs. "Chuckie!" There was no answer. Beaver forgot about not wanting to attract attention. "Chuckie!" he yelled at the top of his voice. Still no answer, but a lot of people stared at Beaver. Boy, thought Beaver, now I'm really in a mess. How would he ever explain this to Wally . . . and his mother and father . . . and Mrs. Murdock?

"Have you seen a little boy in a green sweater?" the clerk asked other clerks and the customers who were trying on shoes. No one had seen Chuckie, but one woman thought she might have seen a little boy walking toward the toy department. She was not sure. There were so many little boys in Mayfield, she saw them everyplace.

"I'll go look," said Beaver, and dodged around the customers to the toy department where once more he called, "Chuckie! Chuckie!"

"Did you lose somebody?" asked a friendly clerk.

"Yes, a little boy about so high." Beaver measured Chuckie's hieght in the air with his hand. "He's wearing a green sweater."

"Why, yes, I saw a lady in children's clothing leading a little boy who was crying toward the accommodation desk," said the clerk. "That's where we take lost children."

"Thanks a lot," said Beaver hastily, thinking at first that the clerk meant the lady was wearing children's clothing and then understanding that she was merely in the children's clothing department. He started dodging through the clusters of customers in the aisles once more before he realized he did not know where the accommodation desk was. Then he discovered he was in the ladies' underwear department and he wasn't going to stop and ask for directions there.

He hurried on to the men's clothing department and

was told that the accommodation desk was at the rear of the store under the balcony. Then Beaver could hear the little boy crying and stopped feeling worried. Poor little Chuckie. He was probably scared to death because he couldn't find Beaver and was all alone in the store and didn't know how he would get home.

When Beaver finally pushed his way through a crowd of women who were looking at a counter piled with sweaters on sale, he reached the accommodation desk and saw the little boy. He wore a red sweater and he was definitely not Chuckie. For a minute Beaver just stood and stared, hoping that somehow the little boy in the red sweater would turn into Chuckie in a green sweater. When he remained a stranger, Beaver wearily made his way back to the shoe department. "Did you find him?" he asked the clerk without much hope.

"No, I haven't," answered the clerk. "I've been all over the store. I am afraid he is lost."

Now Beaver really did not know what to do. He wished Wally were there. Wally always knew what to do in an emergency. He felt through his pockets, hoping to find a dime for a telephone call. He did not have a dime and then he remembered that even if he did have, Wally was not home.

"Why don't you call the little boy's mother?" suggested the clerk. "Perhaps she would know where he might have gone. You may use our phone behind the counter."

"Thanks," said Beaver, and went to the telephone, where he hesitated. Somehow he could not bring himself to telephone Chuckie's mother and say, "I'm sorry but I lost your little boy." He decided he would try telephoning his own house first. If his father had returned he might know what to do.

When Beaver dialed his own number he was surprised when Wally answered. "How come you're home?" Beaver blurted.

"Aw, the manager of the ice rink knows Eddie and wouldn't let us in. He said only his father could use the free passes," explained Wally, and then demanded, "Hey, Beaver, where have you been, anyway?"

"All over," answered Beaver.

"Well, you better come home with Chuckie right away," Wally told him. "Mrs. Murdock will be expecting Chuckie, and Mom and Dad are going to come home pretty soon and start asking questions. They aren't going to like it because I turned the job over to you."

"Wally, I'm in trouble," Beaver confessed. "I can't come home with Chuckie on account of Chuckie's lost."

"You're in trouble! Boy, what do you think I'm in?" Wally sounded angry. "How could you lose Chuckie?"

"I don't know," said Beaver hopelessly. "I just did. I've been looking all over."

"Boy, Beaver, what a mess," said Wally angrily. "You're a dumb little kid."

This made Beaver angry. "Well, it's all your fault for trusting a dumb little kid!"

There was a long silence from Wally on the other end of the telephone. Finally he said, "Look, Beaver, you stay right where you are and keep looking for Chuckie. I'll figure out something." With that he hung up.

Beaver felt a little better because he was sure Wally would think of something.

"Did you make your call?" asked the clerk, who by now was fitting a shoe on a little girl.

"Yes, sir," answered Beaver, and then a terrible thought came to him. He had not told Wally where he was. Wally would not know where to find him or where to telephone him. "Do you mind if I make another call?"

"Not at all," said the busy clerk.

Beaver put his hand on the receiver and paused. He did not like Wally's calling him a dumb little kid one bit. And the reason he did not like it was that he felt like a dumb little kid. His mother would think he was a dumb little kid. His father would think he was a dumb little kid. Mrs. Murdock—well, Beaver did not even like to think about what Mrs. Murdock would think. And then there was the ninety cents Wally wasn't going to collect. The way he had been acting about money lately, he was going to be pretty mad about that, especially after what happened to Nick the horse a couple of weeks ago.

Beaver felt so terrible he didn't want to face any of them again. Not ever. He would just go away and be a hobo or something. He would ride on freight cars and cook things in tin cans over campfires. Then when he was old enough he would join the navy or maybe the French Foreign Legion. That would be better. He would join the French Foreign Legion and ... do whatever they did ... ride around on camels or something ... and then when he was pretty old he would come home in his Foreign Legion uniform and his mother and father would be old and tottery. Wally would be sort of feeble, too. They would all be real poor and he would come home and bring them all a million dollars or something. That would make Wally forget about the ninety cents. He would get his picture on the front page of the paper and everybody would celebrate because he had come back after all those years of being lost.

Beaver had not worked out all the details of exactly what he would do in all those years while the whole family was growing old, but right now he decided to telephone home to say good-bye. When Wally heard he was going away he would be sorry he had called him a dumb little kid.

This time his father answered. "Beaver!" exclaimed Mr. Cleaver. Beaver heard him say to someone in the room at home, "It's Beaver."

Beaver heard his mother answer, "Thank heaven!"

"Dad, I guess you know about Chuckie getting lost," said Beaver, "and I just called to say good-bye."

"Good-bye?" Mr. Cleaver sounded surprised.

"Yes," said Beaver. "I'm going away and I'm never coming back."

"Beaver, what are you talking about?" asked his father.

"Well, a fellow can come home if he just lost a sock or a sweater or something," explained Beaver, "but he can't come home if he loses a whole boy."

"Beaver," said Mr. Cleaver patiently, "Chuckie is home and everything is all right. Now you tell me where you are and I'll come right down and get you."

Beaver was so relieved he felt dazed. Chuckie was home and everything was all right. His father had said so. "I'm still in the shoe department," he managed to say.

"Don't move," said his father. "We'll be right there."

When his father had hung up, Beaver decided his father did not mean he could not sit down. Exhausted, he sank into a chair. "It's O.K.," he told the clerk. "Chuckie's found."

"I'm mighty glad to hear that," said the clerk. "For awhile there I was worried."

While Beaver waited for his father another worry popped into his mind. Chuckie was safe at home, but what about those two pair of shoes? Mrs. Murdock wasn't going to like it if those shoes charged to her account got lost. Beaver felt too tired to settle down to any serious worrying. He just sat until his father appeared.

"Did Chuckie get home with his shoes all right?" he asked when his father came hurrying down the aisle after him.

"Chuckie got home all right," answered Mr. Cleaver. "I don't know about the shoes."

"How did he get home?" Beaver asked curiously.

"Well, it seems he was deliberately hiding from you when he met Mr. Swanson who lives down the street. He told Mr. Swanson that he was downtown alone because you brought him down and then got lost. Naturally Mr. Swanson took him home," explained Mr. Cleaver. "And don't worry. Chuckie's mother gave him a good spanking."

That was not what was worrying Beaver. "I guess you're pretty mad at me, aren't you, Dad?" he asked when he was in the car on the way home.

"Well . . . not exactly, Beaver," said Mr. Cleaver. "It's Wally who did the wrong thing. He had no business taking on a job and then turning it over to you."

"But it was my idea," admitted Beaver.

"That doesn't make any difference," said Mr. Cleaver. "Wally is old enough to know better."

Oh fine, thought Beaver. Now he had got Wally into

trouble, so that meant he would be in trouble with Wally. When Beaver returned home he went upstairs, where he found his brother lying on his bed staring moodily at the ceiling. "It wasn't your fault," Wally told him.

Beaver sat down on the edge of his own bed. "Gee, Wally, it seems like every time I have a good idea, it gets you into trouble. Did Chuckie bring the shoes home?"

"Yeah, he brought them home all right," said Wally. "Both pairs. Now I have to return one pair to the store. And there was such a fuss about Chuckie getting lost that Mrs. Murdock didn't pay the dollar. Not that I expected her to, after everything that happened."

"Gee, Wally, I'll take the other shoes back," said Beaver. "That part really was my fault."

"Oh, no, you don't," said Wally with a rueful grin. "Enough things have gone wrong with this deal already."

"Yeah." Beaver managed to grin himself.

"Just promise not to get any more bright ideas," said Wally.

"I promise," said Beaver, and thought awhile. "Wally, you sure must need money an awful lot for something if you're willing to baby-sit. That's girl's work."

"Oh, I don't know," said Wally. "Some fellows baby-sit. Maybe I would have felt it was girl's work once, but not now. Anyway, you want to know something?" This time Wally's grin was whole-hearted. "When a fellow wins his letter for sports there are a lot of things he doesn't mind doing that he wouldn't have done before."

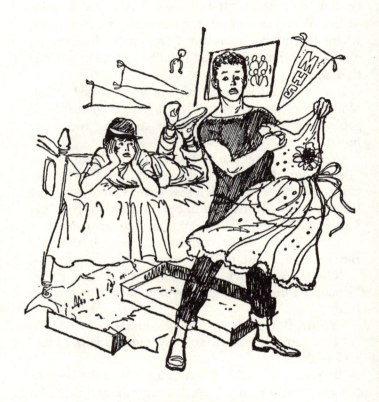

WALLY'S PLAY

It seemed to Beaver that all of a sudden Wally was taking more showers than really necessary and spending a lot of time combing lilac-smelling stuff through his curly hair. Beaver, who let his own brown hair hang down over his forehead any old way, and who took a shower only when his mother reminded him, knew why Wally was doing these things. The reason was girls.

Wally liked girls more than he used to, especially two of them—Mary Ellen Rogers and a girl named Kitty Benson who had once lived in Mayfield and who now lived in Bellport and had been writing to Wally on pink paper ever since he went away to camp the previous summer. Wally even parted with some of the money he had been hoarding and spent it taking Mary Ellen to the movies on Saturday night. He had also taken to answering Kitty's letters right away, which of course only encouraged her to write more often.

Beaver was disappointed in his brother. A fellow like Wally who might even get to be an Olympic track star someday—it was really too bad. Besides, Beaver always enjoyed bragging about Wally at school, and if he was going to waste his time on girls he wouldn't have anything to brag about.

Beaver could not help hoping something would happen to make Wally forget all this girl nonsense and stop washing so much. That was why he listened with such interest one day before supper when he heard his mother say to his father, "Ward, would you make a little fuss over Wally at supper?"

"What's up?" asked Mr. Cleaver.

"He got elected to a club called the Crusaders at high school," answered Mrs. Cleaver. "They took in only ten sophomores, so it's quite an honor."

"What kind of a club is this?" Mr. Cleaver wanted to know.

"It's the letterman's club," explained Mrs. Cleaver. "The school sponsors it and they put on plays and things."

"Fine." Mr. Cleaver sounded pleased. "I'll make the same kind of fuss I did when he brought up his mark in Spanish—a B-plus type of fuss."

Beaver thought the Crusaders sounded like a good club. There wouldn't be any girls in it and Wally wouldn't have any reason to wash. It might even take his mind off Mary Ellen Rogers and that Kitty Benson and her pink letters.

At the table that evening Mr. Cleaver turned to his oldest son. "Well, Wally, I understand you made the Crusaders at school. That's quite an honor."

"Yeah, it's a real neat club, Dad," said Wally, looking pleased. "I don't know why they took me. They usually just take the swingers."

Beaver grinned. "He's just saying that, Dad, so you'll tell him what a neat guy he is."

"He is a neat guy," said Mr. Cleaver. "Who else in your class was invited to join, Wally?"

"Eddie Haskell was the only other fellow from my home room," said Wally. "He was assistant manager of the basketball team and in the middle of the season the real manager got the mumps, so they had to give him his letter."

"I don't know why, but somehow that sounds like Eddie," remarked Mr. Cleaver.

"Yeah, leave it to Eddie to get in somehow," agreed Beaver. Eddie was what Wally and his friends called a sharp operator. He always managed to get the most out of any situation with the least amount of work.

Wally laughed. "That isn't all. When Eddie ordered new jerseys he spelled Crusaders wrong. He spelled it O-R-S instead of E-R-S and the team had to wear them wrong side out till we could get them changed."

"What activities do the Crusaders have planned?" asked Mr. Cleaver.

"In a couple of weeks we're going to put on the

Crusader Follies. The fellows do it every year," explained Wally.

"What are they going to do in the Follies?" asked Beaver, who was always curious about the things that went on in high school. Someday he would go there himself, even though at the moment it seemed a hundred years away.

"They're going to do a take-off on a Western play," said Wally.

Beaver was glad to hear this. A Western put on by a bunch of fellows should keep Wally away from girls for awhile. "With cowboys and shooting?" he asked, just to make sure.

"I guess with cowboys and shooting," answered Wally. "I just got in the Crusaders, so they'll probably give me a part where I stand around while the other fellows say things. Duke Hathaway—he's the head of it—said we'll get our parts and costumes tomorrow."

"Gee, Duke Hathaway." Beaver was impressed. Duke Hathaway's picture had been in the sport section almost every week during the basketball season.

"Haven't I heard that name someplace?" asked Mr. Cleaver.

"Sure. The Duke made all-state guard in basketball again this year," said Wally. "He sort of pushes people around, but he's O.K., I guess."

So Wally was going to be in a Western with Duke Hathaway. This was something Beaver could tell the other boys at school. They would be pretty impressed, because everyone knew about Duke Hathaway.

The next afternoon Beaver was in the kitchen turning the handle of the meat grinder for his mother when Wally came home from school carrying his books and a large suit box. "Hi, Wally," said Beaver. "We're grinding up cow for supper. What's in the box?"

"Nothing," answered Wally flatly.

"I'll bet it's your costume for the play," said Beaver. "I told all the kids at school how you were going to be a cowboy in a play with Duke Hathaway. *The* Duke Hathaway."

"What did you have to go and do that for?" Wally asked crossly.

"Because your brother is proud of you," said Mrs. Cleaver. "Wouldn't you like to show us your costume?"

"No, thank you." Wally sounded bitter as he left the room. Beaver heard him climbing the stairs with a heavy tread instead of running up two at a time as he so often did.

Beaver ground the rest of the meat in a hurry and followed Wally upstairs to the bedroom. There he found his brother lying on his bed staring at the ceiling, which was better than finding him washing or combing his hair. "Hey, how about letting me see the costume you brought home for the play?" Beaver asked eagerly. "Are you a Good Guy or a Bad Guy?"

"I'm not letting you see it." Wally sounded as if he meant what he said.

"Where is it?" asked Beaver.

"Never mind," said Wally angrily. "I don't want you putting your grubby hands on it."

"My hands aren't grubby," said Beaver indignantly. "Mom made me wash them before I ground the meat."

Wally scowled at the ceiling. "Even if you washed them a hundred times they would still be grubby."

Beaver was baffled. This was not like Wally. "Gee, Wally, what's bothering you?"

Wally sat up and glared at Beaver. "Nothing is bothering me and stop picking on me."

"O.K., O.K., if that's the way you feel about it."
Now it was Beaver's turn to be angry. He stalked out
of the room. Let Wally sit there and scowl if he wanted
to. Beaver didn't care. Wally needn't think that just
because he was a Crusader and in a play with Duke
Hathaway he was too good to associate with his own
family. He could keep his old costume, if that was the
way he felt about it. It was probably just a pair of old
chaps made out of imitation leather. Anyway, there
was nothing about a cowboy costume that could make
Wally act this way, so it must be a girl who was up-
setting him. Maybe Mary Ellen Rogers had let Eddie
Haskell walk home from school with her. Or maybe
Wally was expecting one of those pink letters from
Kitty Benson and it hadn't come. It was too bad.

Beaver did not give Wally's costume another thought
until the next afternoon, when he was looking for his
baseball. He looked in the drawers and in the closet
and then he chanced to look under Wally's bed where
he found, not a baseball, but the suit box. He pulled it
out and looked at it. This was Wally's costume for the
play. Beaver started to remove the lid to see what was
inside and then he changed his mind. That would be
snooping.

Beaver went on searching for his baseball but he
could not get that box out of his mind. It was probably
just a cowboy suit . . . but it must be an awfully funny-
looking one if Wally took such pains to hide it.

Finally Beaver could stand it no longer. He would
take one peek, a quick one. Wally had no reason to be-
have the way he did. Beaver lifted one end of the lid
and what he saw surprised him so that he snatched the
lid all the way off the box and stared.

The box was filled with red material, some of it

shiny and some of it thin and all of it trimmed with little round glittery things. He lifted out the material and discovered that it was a dress, the kind of dress he had seen ladies that danced in saloons wear on television. "Wow!" said Beaver to himself. Then he discovered a pair of high-heeled slippers in the box. This was the funniest looking cowboy costume he had ever seen, and this was what Wally was going to wear in the play!

Beaver stepped into the high-heeled shoes and held the dress up in front of himself before the mirror. Wally had to wear this in front of the whole school! It was the funniest thing Beaver had ever heard of. He began to laugh. He laughed so hard he fell over the bed with the dress clutched to his chest. Old Wally dancing around like a saloon lady! Boy!

Wally's voice cut his laughter short. "All right, wise guy," he said from the doorway.

"Oh, hello, Wally," said Beaver weakly.

"You little sneak." Wally was really angry. "Didn't I tell you to keep your grubby hands off my stuff?"

"I wasn't looking for it, Wally. I just happened to find it by accident," Beaver tried to explain.

"You little rat," said Wally in disgust. "I'm telling you, Beaver, if you say anything about this to anybody, I'm going to fix you good." Wally looked as threatening as he sounded.

"Don't worry, Wally," Beaver assured him, suddenly sobered by the thought that Miss Landers' room might hear about this. "I'd be ashamed to tell anybody my brother was a girl." Because he knew it would annoy Wally, he held the dress up in front of the mirror and simpered at his reflection.

"Let me have that," yelled Wally furiously, as he snatched at the dress.

"Stop pushing me around," Beaver yelled back. He held onto the dress.

Wally grabbed the flimsy material and jerked. The dress ripped completely down the back. "Now look what you did!" said Wally, even more furiously. "This costume belongs to the Crusaders and now I'll probably have to pay for it. Why can't you learn to keep your nose out of my business?"

"I don't care!" yelled Beaver. "Girl! Girl! Girl!"

Both Mr. and Mrs. Cleaver appeared in the doorway of the boys' room. "Here, here, boys, what's going on?" asked their father.

"I'm going to clop him," said Wally. "He ripped my dress."

"Your dress?" Mrs. Cleaver did not understand.

"Aw, it's just his crummy costume for the play," explained Beaver.

Mrs. Cleaver picked up the costume. "Wally, why would your costume be a dress?"

"Because he's going to be a girl, that's why," said Beaver, and put his hand over his mouth to stifle a laugh.

Mrs. Cleaver looked questioningly at Wally.

"Yeah," admitted Wally. "The Crusaders are just fellows and they have to play all the parts. Somebody has to play a dancehall girl and they stuck me with it and I'm not going to do it."

"Now wait a minute, Wally," said Mr. Cleaver. "Didn't some of the fellows play girls last year?"

"Yeah. They had a whole chorus line," admitted Wally.

"Well, that's it, Wally," said Mr. Cleaver. "The

whole idea is to horse around and have some fun."

"I don't want to have fun in a girl's dress," protested Wally.

"Yeah," agreed Beaver. "What would my friends say —my brother playing a girl?"

"Now, Wally, we did this kind of thing at college in my fraternity," said Mr. Cleaver. "What are the fellows going to think of you if you won't go along with the spirit of the thing? It's all part of being a Crusader."

"Oh, come on, Wally," said Mrs. Cleaver. "You slip this on and I'll see if I can't sew it up."

"Well, maybe," said Wally gloomily. With great reluctance he pulled the torn dress over his T-shirt and trousers, while his mother found her pincushion. Beaver started to look around for something in the tissue paper in the box.

"You keep out of there," said Wally.

"I just want to see what kind of underwear they gave you," Beaver said, and grinned at Wally.

"Cut that out, will you!" said Wally furiously as he yanked the dress up over his shoulders.

Mrs. Cleaver pinned the ripped material together. "Take a few steps, Wally," she directed. "I want to see how it hangs in back."

"He sure looks pretty, doesn't he?" asked Beaver wickedly. He was having a good time teasing Wally here at home, even though he would never admit to anyone outside his family what had happened.

"That does it!" stormed Wally, pulling the dress off. "I'll quit the Crusaders. I'll quit the school. I'll even quit the whole town if I have to."

"Wally!" cried Mrs. Cleaver. "Now I'll have to pin the dress all over again."

Things were pretty tense around the Cleaver household for the rest of the afternoon. Once when Beaver was in the bathroom he heard Wally talking to himself. He peeked out and saw his brother standing in front of the mirror saying earnestly, "This is the way it is, Duke. The Crusaders are a neat bunch but my studies come first and I shall not be able to accept this part." Then he said to himself in the mirror, "Nah, that's no good."

At the supper table Wally was silent. He chewed thoughtfully as if his mind were someplace else. Then suddenly, along about dessert time, he stopped looking thoughtful. He smiled, joined in the conversation and asked for a second helping of pie.

Now what's he up to, wondered Beaver, and asked for a second helping of pie himself. Actually he hoped Wally had found a way to get out of the part. He did not want his own friends to find out about it, which they were almost sure to do because some of them had brothers and sisters in high school, too. This was the kind of news that traveled fast.

The next afternoon Beaver and Wally happened to come home at the same time and met in front of their house. Wally was looking thoughtful again, so Beaver knew that whatever plan he had had to get out of being a dancehall girl had not worked. "Practice the play today?" he asked.

"Nah," muttered Wally and then, seeing Eddie Haskell coming down the street, he suddenly looked happier. "Hi, Eddie," he called.

"Well, if it isn't Beaver and the Queen of the Dance-hall Girls," said Eddie, with one of his smirking laughs.

To Beaver's surprise Wally grinned amiably and said, "What are you laughing at, Eddie?"

"I was just thinking of you clomping around on the

stage in that dress in front of the whole school and all their parents and brothers and sisters. Practically the whole town," said Eddie. "And in high heels too, you and your big feet."

Wally took this calmly. "Oh? Duke Hathaway tells me it's the biggest part in the play."

Eddie's smile was not quite so broad. "You mean you got a lot of lines?"

"About eight pages," said Wally.

Beaver, impressed by his brother's strategy, decided to help Wally out. "Mary Ellen Rogers said she might come over and coach him. She might come over a couple of nights a week," he said, knowing that Eddie also liked Mary Ellen.

"Oh," was all Eddie had to say.

"Yeah, that's what she said," Wally sounded as if what Beaver had said was true. "How many lines do you have in the play, Eddie?"

"Well, I say, 'Here comes the sheriff' and later on I say, 'Somebody stole our horses.'" Eddie had nothing to brag about.

"Gee, you know your part already, Eddie," Beaver said. "You're not going to need any coaching from girls or anything."

Wally laid a consoling hand on Eddie's shoulder. "Well, I guess they'll like your two lines as much as if you had a real part." Then he turned to his brother. "Hey, Beav, you want to throw a football around after supper?"

"Yeah, I'd like to throw a football after supper," said Beaver, feeling that he and Wally were showing good teamwork in front of Eddie.

Something was bothering Eddie. "Hey, Wally . . . do you really not mind being a girl in the play?"

"A fellow has to get in the spirit of things when he's in a club like the Crusaders, doesn't he?" asked Wally. "You know, horse around and have a lot of fun."

Now it was Beaver's turn. "Wally, my whole class is coming. Will you give them your autograph?"

"Sure," agreed Wally. "Why should I be stuck up?"

Eddie was still bothered by something. "Say, Wally, tell me something. How come the Duke gave you such a good part?"

"I guess the Duke wanted to give it to a swinger," said Wally modestly.

"The Duke thinks you're a swinger?" asked Eddie.

"Well, he gave me the part, didn't he?" said Wally. "Hey, Beaver, you want to throw the football around now?"

"Yeah, I'd like to throw the football around now," agreed Beaver.

"Would you excuse us, Eddie?" said Wally. "We're going to throw the football around."

"Yeah, sure," said Eddie. "I have to be going anyway. See you around."

"Do you think he fell for it?" asked Wally, as soon as Eddie was out of earshot.

"I don't know," said Beaver. "I sure hope so. Do you really want to throw the football, Wally?"

"Heck no," said Wally, and went into the house.

Beaver was not disappointed. He had not expected Wally to want to throw the football. Anyway he was more interested in finding out whether or not the scheme worked.

That evening after supper when Wally was upstairs studying and the rest of the family was watching television, the doorbell rang. "I'll get it," said Mr. Cleaver.

"Good evening, Mr. Cleaver," said a boy who,

Beaver could see from his chair, was slightly older and much bigger than Wally and who was wearing a letterman's sweater with three stripes. "I'm Harold Hathaway. I wonder if I could see Wally."

Duke Hathaway in person! Right here in the Cleaver's front hall!

"He's doing his homework," said Mr. Cleaver, as calmly as if the Duke were not just about the most important person in Mayfield. "Why don't you go on up to his room?"

Beaver couldn't wait until the visitor climbed the stairs. He heard Wally say as if he were surprised, "Oh . . . hi, Duke." Then he heard the bedroom door close. "Dad!" exclaimed Beaver. "That was Duke Hathaway. Right here in our house!"

"My, aren't we lucky," remarked Mrs. Cleaver dryly as she turned down the television set. "Ward, why did they close the door?"

"Because they didn't want us to hear them," answered Mr. Cleaver. "Don't you think it would look better if you turned up the TV again?"

"Why didn't they want us to hear them?" wondered Mrs. Cleaver, ignoring her husband's suggestion.

"Because we are parents," explained Mr. Cleaver.

Beaver wished his parents would be quiet because Wally and the Duke might say something loud enough to be heard through the door. He started silently up the stairs so that he might hear better.

"Beaver, come back here," said Mr. Cleaver. "You have no business trying to eavesdrop on your brother and his friend."

"Gee, Dad," protested Beaver, descending the stairs. "I only want to know what they're talking about."

"Me, too," said Mrs. Cleaver. "It isn't every day we have a real swinger come to call."

Beaver sat in front of the television set without seeing a thing. He was too busy wondering what the Duke wanted to see Wally about. Maybe the Duke was going to resign as president of the Crusaders and wanted Wally to take over. Or maybe it was something about the play. That was it, of course. But what about the play? Beaver could not wait to find out.

In a few minutes Wally and his visitor came out of the room and as they started down the stairs Beaver heard the Duke say, "Big of you to see it this way, Cleaver. The Crusaders won't forget what you've done." He spoke pleasantly to Mr. and Mrs. Cleaver from the hall and said goodnight to Wally.

"What did he want?" demanded Beaver, the instant the door was closed behind the Duke.

"Yes," said Mrs. Cleaver. "What did you and the swinger talk about?"

Wally shrugged. "Well, Eddie Haskell went over to see the Duke this afternoon and whined around so the Duke came over to see if I'd do the Crusaders a big favor by letting Eddie play the dancehall girl instead of me."

"Boy, oh, boy!" shouted Beaver. "It worked! Old Eddie really fell for it!" For once he had not spoiled something for Wally the way he had when he brought the horse home from the carnival and when he lost Chuckie in the shoe department. This time he had been a help to Wally.

"You mean you're out of the play?" Mr. Cleaver sounded as if he did not approve.

"No, I got another part," said Wally.

"Fine," said Mr. Cleaver. "If you like we'll help you with your lines."

Wally grinned half-heartedly. "I know them already, Dad. All I say is 'Here comes the sheriff' and 'Somebody stole our horses.' " Then he went back upstairs to study.

It suddenly struck Beaver that something was wrong. Wally was not behaving as he should. He should have acted pleased instead of smiling half-heartedly and walking up the stairs as if his feet were too heavy to carry.

"I don't think that's a very good television program," remarked Beaver, and followed Wally up to their room. "How come you aren't happy?" he asked his brother. "You got out of being a girl and that's what you wanted, isn't it?"

Wally made a face. "Aw . . . it didn't really work out the way I figured it would at all."

"What do you mean, it didn't work out?" demanded Beaver. "You wanted to get out of being a girl and you got out of being a girl. Now all the fellows can laugh at Eddie instead of you."

"I suppose so," said Wally, sitting down at his desk and picking up his pen. "But wouldn't you know? Mary Ellen Rogers really is going to help Eddie with his lines. He asked her and she said yes, anything to help out a Crusader. Every day after school until he learns them. And he has eight pages to learn and if I know that Eddie Haskell it's going to take him a long, long time to learn them."

Beaver sat down on the bed with a thump. "Gee, Wally . . . I guess it was my fault. I shouldn't have made up that stuff about Mary Ellen Rogers coaching you."

"Aw, skip it," said Wally gloomily. "Eddie probably would have thought of it anyway."

"I'm sure sorry, Wally," said Beaver.

"I got out of the part, didn't I?" said Wally. "But try to remember what I said about not getting any more bright ideas."

"I'll sure work at it," agreed Beaver. And he really meant it.

WALLY, THE LIFEGUARD

On Wednesday afternoons Wally was always late getting home from school because he had to stay to practice for track. On one Wednesday he was unusually late, so late that Mr. Cleaver was already home when he arrived. Wally came bursting through the back door and flung his books on the kitchen table. "Hey, guess what?" he said to his family. "I got a job!"

"Another?" said Mrs. Cleaver.

Beaver reminded himself that no matter what Wally's job was, he was not going to get mixed up in it. He had caused Wally enough trouble and besides, he had promised.

"I'm going to be a lifeguard up at Friend's Lake on Saturdays," Wally went on enthusiastically. "I'm going to get ten dollars a day and free meals thrown in and get to wear a uniform and they're going to take out withholding and everything."

"What's withholding?" asked Beaver.

"It's the money they take out of your salary to run the government," Wally explained.

"Gee, I didn't know that they took money away from kids to run the government." Somehow it did not seem fair to Beaver.

"Sure. Even if you're a baby and you earn money, they'll take out withholding." Wally turned to his father. "What's the matter, Dad? You've got that look on your face like you're going to say no."

"Well, I do think you should slow down a minute," said Mr. Cleaver. "Where did this job come from?"

"It comes from three college fellows that can't start working until school is out. The man who owns the lake needs someone who lives close enough to come up Saturdays for a few week ends, so he called the coach at high school and he recommended three of his best swimmers and that was me and two seniors," Wally explained.

Beaver was almost as enthusiastic as Wally. "Boy, this is going to be neat. We're going to be the only family I know that has its own lifeguard right in it." And wouldn't this be something to tell the kids at school! Wally a real lifeguard!

"Well, it's quite an honor to be recommended by the coach," admitted Mr. Cleaver.

"But Ward, it's such a responsibility for a boy Wally's age," protested Mrs. Cleaver.

"The coach wouldn't have picked him unless he thought he could do the job," Mr. Cleaver pointed out. "And it will only be a few week ends till school is out."

Mrs. Cleaver was still not convinced. "Well, if you think so, Ward. But I want you to talk to the man up there and be sure he doesn't let Wally do anything dangerous."

"All right, dear," answered Mr. Cleaver with a grin. "I'll tell him just to have Wally rescue people in shallow water."

"Yipee!" Wally tossed a book into the air and caught it. "Now I can afford to take Mary Ellen Rogers to the dance at the country club."

"Oh, that reminds me," said Mrs. Cleaver. "There is another letter from Kitty Benson for you on the hall table."

"Take Mary Ellen Rogers to the dance at the country club!" echoed Beaver. "What do you need a lot of money to do that for?"

"Aw, you wouldn't understand," said Wally. "It costs a lot of money to take a girl someplace special like that. You have to buy her a flower—an orchid or something —and you have to take her someplace extra-fancy to eat and that costs a lot of money. You can't expect a girl wearing an orchid to eat a hot dog. And if she is eating something fancy, you can't expect me to sit there eating a hot dog."

"I like hot dogs," said Beaver.

At least he now knew that Wally was not in need of money because he was in some kind of trouble, but to want to earn money just so a girl could wear an orchid and eat up a lot of expensive food seemed like a waste to him. There were lots of good things Wally could buy for the price of an orchid. Oh well, if Wally wanted to waste his money on orchids, that was his business. And in the meantime Beaver could tell everyone at school that his brother was going to be a lifeguard at Friend's Lake. Or maybe he wouldn't brag. He would wait until Wally rescued somebody and got his picture on the front page of the paper. Then when everyone said, "Gee, Beaver, was that your brother who had his picture in the paper?" he would just smile modestly and say yes.

However, Beaver could not keep from bragging. The first thing he did was telephone Gilbert and Whitey and tell them all about it, leaving out of course the part about the orchid. They were both properly impressed and said they were going to try to go to the lake the next Saturday just to see Wally at work as a lifeguard. Neither boy had ever known a real lifeguard before. Beaver asked his friends not to telephone a lot of people and tell them the news. He wanted dibs on bragging about his own brother.

Friday afternoon Wally came home from school with a large paper bag.

"What do you have there?" asked Mrs. Cleaver.

"Just my lifeguard hat and junk," said Wally. "I bought it from the brother of a college fellow who used to be a lifeguard up at the lake last summer. It's kind of second-hand looking but he only charged me three dollars because his brother is away at school."

"Maybe your father can buy you a new outfit," suggested Mrs. Cleaver.

"Oh no, Mom." Wally did not like the idea. "This

stuff is all broken in. I don't want to look like a new
lifeguard. And I brought a paper for Dad to sign that
says it's O.K. with him for me to take the job."

"Put your lifeguard suit on, Wally," begged Beaver.

"Heck no," said Wally. "What if the neighbors saw
me walking around the house in broad daylight? They'd
think I'd flipped or something."

"Tonight, then?" coaxed Beaver.

"Maybe," said Wally.

Beaver did not let his brother forget, and after supper persuaded Wally to try on his lifeguard outfit by
promising to let him practice artificial respiration on
him. He felt pretty proud when Wally appeared in his
white boxer trunks, a T-shirt with "Friend's Lake Lifeguard" painted across the front and a white helmet
with "Lifeguard" painted on it in big red letters.
"Doesn't he look neat, huh, Mom?" asked Beaver.

"He certainly does," agreed Mrs. Cleaver. "If I were
a sweet little high-school girl, I couldn't wait to be
saved by him."

This was something that had not occurred to Beaver.
Naturally a lot of girls were going to hang around a
good-looking fellow like Wally. Oh well, if Wally was
willing to work to earn money just to waste on an orchid there was no point in worrying about him. He was
too far gone already.

Beaver and Wally had just gone upstairs to their
room when Eddie Haskell came over and joined them.

"He looks like a real lifeguard, doesn't he, Eddie?"
said Beaver proudly.

"Sure he does," agreed Eddie. "I get your angle,
Wally. I can see those girls now saying, 'Oh, save me,
save me, Mr. Lifeguard. I am drowning, glub-glub-
glub.' "

"Ah, cut it out, Eddie," said Wally, but Beaver could see he did not mind being teased.

"Well, come on, Tarzan," said Eddie. "Get out of that outfit and let's go to the movies."

"What's playing?" asked Wally.

"Who cares?" asked Eddie. "It's Friday night."

Wally thought it over. "No, I think I better get to bed early. I've got to get up pretty early to catch the bus to Friend's Lake."

Eddie gave him a playful slap on the back. "Yeah, well, get your beauty rest, Champ."

"Hey, Wally," said Beaver when Eddie had gone. "How come Eddie doesn't care what's playing at the movies?"

"Beaver, didn't you ever hear of girls?" asked Wally.

"Hear of them?" said Beaver in disgust. "I wish they had never been invented." He had been forced to have Violet Rutherford for a partner in folk dancing that day at school.

Wally was so anxious not to miss the bus to Friend's Lake that he set two alarm clocks, one that went off half an hour before he left and the other that went off about fifteen minutes after he had gone. This resulted in the whole Cleaver family getting up earlier than usual. At breakfast Mr. Cleaver made a suggestion. "Maybe a little later on this morning we could drive up to Friend's Lake. Beaver might enjoy an outing."

"Hey, that would be keen, Dad," agreed Beaver enthusiastically. "We would get to see Wally lifeguarding. I know, I'll take my camera along and take his picture right there while he's guarding people's lives."

"Yes, and I can pack a lunch," suggested Mrs. Cleaver. "That way Wally won't think we came up there just to watch him."

Beaver was happy to start off on an expedition to Friend's Lake, his favorite picnic spot. The lake was large enough for both swimming and fishing. There were plenty of picnic tables and a good sandy beach for sun-bathing or playing ball. When the Cleavers reached the lake shortly before noon, they found the parking lot crowded and they had to walk around through the picnic grounds before they found a vacant table. While Mrs. Cleaver unpacked the lunch and Mr. Cleaver hunted for a piece of wood to put under one of the legs to keep the table from tipping, Beaver went off in search of Wally. He took the camera along to record the sight of Wally guarding the lives of the swimmers at Friend's Lake.

When Beaver reached the beach, he headed for the first lifeguard stand, a high platform where the lifeguard could sit under a beach umbrella and see over the beach and the lake. Beaver aimed the camera, hoping to surprise his brother. "Hey, Wally!" Beaver called.

A strange lifeguard turned around. "You want something, kid?" he asked.

"Oh . . . no," answered Beaver, letting the camera hang on the strap around his neck. "I'm looking for my brother and you aren't him."

"Maybe he's on the next stand," suggested the lifeguard.

"Maybe." Beaver made his way through the sun-bathers on the beach to the second lifeguard who, he saw immediately, was not Wally. "Say, do you know where I can find Wally Cleaver? He's a lifeguard here."

"Wally Cleaver?" said the lifeguard. "Try one of the other stands."

Wally had to be on the next stand. Beaver plodded through the sand until he came to the last lifeguard stand. This guard was not Wally either. Beaver thought this was mighty peculiar. He wondered if Wally had taken the wrong bus and got lost.

"Say, do you know my brother, Wally Cleaver?" Beaver inquired of the guard.

"Wally? Sure I know Wally," said the guard. "We go to school together."

"Have you seen him around here?" asked Beaver.

"Yeah, I saw him the first thing this morning," said the guard. "He was wearing a lifeguard helmet and talking to Mr. Burton, the boss, but I don't think I've seen him since. He must be around someplace."

"Well . . . thanks," said Beaver, and then thought that as long as he was talking to a lifeguard, he might as well ask another question. "Say, if a dog falls in the lake do you have to save him, too?"

"It's never come up," answered the guard.

"Would you have to save a monkey?" persisted Beaver.

"Just people," answered the guard. "You run along and find your brother. I'm supposed to be watching the swimmers."

Beaver did not know where to look for his brother. He knew that Wally had arrived at Friend's Lake with his lifeguard helmet and he knew that Wally was not occupying any of the lifeguard stands. So where could he be? In the lake? Maybe Wally had reported for work and jumped in to save someone the very first thing and drowned himself. Beaver could not take this thought seriously. If Wally jumped in to save someone, he would save him and not go glub-glub-glub to the bottom of the lake himself. Beaver decided to tell his father that he could not find Wally and perhaps his father could find Mr. Burton, the owner of the lake, and ask where Wally was.

As Beaver was plodding through the sand back to the picnic table he was vaguely aware of someone shouting, "Get your cold drinks. Get your red-hots!" It seemed to him that it was Wally shouting, but of course that was impossible. Still the voice continued. "Get your cold drinks, get your red-hots. We got 'em, you want 'em. Look here, look here!"

It was Wally's voice. There was no mistaking it. Beaver did not know what to think. He turned and looked across the sun bathers and sure enough, there was Wally wearing a chef's hat with "Red Hots" printed across the front and carrying a tray of soft drinks and hot dogs supported by a strap around his neck. "Get your cold drinks, get your red-hots," Wally called out, but Beaver could tell he was not very happy about it. "We got 'em, you want 'em. Look here, look here."

This was awful—Wally selling hot dogs when he was supposed to be saving lives. It was embarrassing. Everybody in Mayfield would see him. Something terrible had gone wrong with Wally's plans. For a minute Beaver wondered if in some way he was responsible— he had upset Wally's plans so many times—but after thinking it over he was sure he could not be to blame this time. Something unexpected must have happened, or maybe Wally forgot his swimming trunks. Beaver had to find out what happened so he plodded back through the sand to Wally. "Hi," he said to his brother.

"Hi," said Wally unhappily, as he opened a bottle of soda pop and handed it to a girl. "What are you doing here?"

"Mom and Dad and I came up for a picnic," explained Beaver. Wally looked so discouraged Beaver tried to hide his own disappointment. "How come you're doing this?" he asked.

"Aw, when I brought Mr. Burton that paper that Dad had to sign he discovered I wasn't old enough to be a lifeguard. He couldn't help it. It's a state law that says you have to be eighteen." Wally shifted his tray to ease the weight on his back. "As long as I was here he offered me this job just for today. I still get ten dollars," said Wally, but Beaver could see it was not the same as being a lifeguard.

Beaver tried to make a joke. "Well, anyway, you won't have all those pretty girls throwing their arms around your neck when they go glub-glub-glub." His joke did not go over very well.

"No, I guess not," said Wally, looking out over the swimmers in the lake.

"And you can still buy Mary Ellen Rogers that flower and all that fancy food," he reminded Wally, even though he still considered this a waste of money.

Wally brightened at this. "Yeah, that's right," he said, "if she'll go with me. Maybe she'll want to go with Eddie Haskell. They've spent so much time together lately."

Beaver was indignant at the idea that any girl would not jump at the chance to go anyplace with Wally. Of course she would go.

"Get your cold drinks, get your red-hots," Wally called out.

Not knowing what else to do, Beaver followed along beside Wally and watched him serve hot dogs with mustard and relish and take the tops off soft-drink bottles. The beach was crowded and business was good. Wally soon had to go back to Mr. Burton for another supply of hot dogs and on the way he had to pass the Cleavers' picnic table.

"Why, Wally!" exclaimed Mrs. Cleaver in astonishment.

"What happened, son?" asked Mr. Cleaver.

Briefly and miserably Wally explained what had happened.

"Well now, Wally, don't be too upset," said Mr. Cleaver. "It's a compliment to you that your swimming was good enough for the job, even though the law says you're too young. And I admire you for taking on this job even though you're disappointed."

"Thanks, Dad," said Wally, without much spirit, and went on his way to get another load of hot dogs.

Beaver had nothing better to do than tag along and, somewhat to his surprise, Wally, who sometimes did not like to have his younger brother tag after him, did not object. Perhaps he was too discouraged to care. Beaver did not know. And at least, Beaver told himself, this time he was not the cause of Wally's difficulties.

Then he heard a girl's voice. "Why, it's Wally Cleaver!" It was Mary Ellen Rogers.

Beaver and Wally turned in the direction of the voice. Mary Ellen, her friend Alma, and Eddie Haskell were sunning themselves on beach towels. Eddie, who was wearing a calypso straw hat, was pounding on some bongo drums while the girls rubbed suntan oil on their shoulders. "Oh, hi . . ." Wally was both surprised and embarrassed. "I'm . . . uh . . . selling hot dogs."

Mary Ellen and Alma began to giggle. Beaver was disgusted. They were just as bad as Judy Hensler and Violet Rutherford in his room at school. You would think girls in high school would be old enough to know better.

"Eddie told us you were a lifeguard," said Mary Ellen when she had controlled her giggles. "That's why we came up here—to see you be a lifeguard."

"Yeah, what happened?" asked Eddie.

"Aw, they got a law and I'm not old enough," said Wally. "That's why I'm doing this."

"Oh, it's a neat job, Wally," said Eddie in that annoying way of his as he beat out an intricate rhythm on his bongo drums.

"I think you look cute in your hot-dog suit," said Mary Ellen, and began to giggle again.

"Just darling," agreed Alma, and the two girls went off into a gale of giggles.

Wally's face turned bright red and he looked angry, something unusual for good-natured Wally. "Well . . . excuse me. I've got to get back to work." He walked away from his friends and began to call out, "Get your cold drinks, get your red hots."

"There's no use drowning today, girls," said Eddie as Wally left.

"Gee, you look pretty mad, Wally," said Beaver.

"I sure am," snapped Wally. "That Mary Ellen Rogers laughing at me when I was trying to earn money to take her to a dance. Well, after that I wouldn't take her to the dance for a million dollars. I wouldn't even take her to a dog fight, not even if it was just across the street."

"No kidding?" asked Beaver.

"No kidding."

Beaver felt a great admiration for his older brother. He was right. No boy should stand for a girl's laughing at him when he was working. He watched Wally shift the heavy tray of hot dogs and soft drinks to ease the weight on his neck once more, and was proud of Wally. He was also reminded of the camera strap around his own neck.

"Hey, Wally, stand still a minute," Beaver directed, opening the camera. "I want to take your picture."

"What for?" demanded Wally. "So you can show my picture to people for laughs?"

"Jeepers, no," said Beaver, peering into the finder. "I was just thinking. I'm the only guy in Miss Landers' room—in the whole school—who has a brother who sells hot dogs."

Wally seemed pleased. At least he managed a faint smile when he posed with his tray of wares.

Beaver snapped his picture. "Who are you going to take to the dance?" he asked curiously.

"I don't know," said Wally. "Nobody, I guess."

"What about Kitty Benson?" Beaver persisted.

"Aw, I couldn't ask her." Wally went on calling out his wares.

"Then why don't you quit?" asked Beaver. "You won't need a lot of money for orchids and stuff if you aren't going to the dance."

"I'll finish out the day if this strap doesn't saw my neck in two," said Wally. "Mr. Burton is counting on me, and ten dollars will come in handy sometime."

"You know, Wally, I was just thinking something else," said Beaver, as he wound the film in his camera. "Maybe sometime while you're on the beach selling hot dogs, all the lifeguards will be out rescuing other people and there'll be a girl and she'll start drowning. And you'll throw away your hot dogs and swim out and save her in front of all the people."

"Cut it out, Beaver." Wally managed his old smile

once more, so Beaver knew he was feeling better. "You know that's not going to happen."

"Yeah, I know it," agreed Beaver. "And even if you did, on account of you're not eighteen, you'd have to throw her back."

This time Wally really did laugh.

BEAVER'S ACCORDION

Beaver could not understand Wally's behavior after the day he sold hot dogs instead of guarding lives at Friend's Lake. He realized that Wally was disappointed in Mary Ellen for laughing at him, but he could not see why Wally wasted so much time moping around the house. One evening Beaver caught him writing a long letter to Kitty Benson when he should have been studying.

"How come you write to her all the time?" Beaver asked. "You hardly even spoke to her when she lived in Mayfield."

"I guess she's what you might call a pen pal," Wally explained. "I got started writing to her last summer when I was at camp and all the other fellows were getting letters from girls."

"What do you write about?" Beaver was curious. He could not imagine what he could ever find to say to a girl in a letter.

"Oh . . . stuff," said Wally vaguely.

"What kind of stuff?" persisted Beaver.

"Let me alone, will you?" snapped Wally. "Can't a fellow have a little peace in his own house once in a while?"

"It's my own house, too," Beaver reminded his brother, and lapsed into an injured silence. Just because Wally wasn't taking Mary Ellen Rogers to a dumb old dance was no reason to go around growling at everybody. He should be happy. Look at the money he was saving.

Wally seemed more cheerful one Saturday when his father suggested he help paint the patio furniture. Beaver watched him gather up rags and brushes in preparation for the job, and then he joined his father and brother in the backyard where they started the job by washing and sanding down the furniture. This looked like hard work, so Beaver did not offer to help.

"Say, Dad, how come we have to wash down the furniture and sand it before we paint it?" Wally asked.

"If we do it this way, the paint job will last for two or three years," Mr. Cleaver explained.

"Yeah, but what if Mom gets tired of the color in

a year?" asked Beaver. "Then you'll have to do it all over again."

Mr. Cleaver smiled. "Well, Beaver, in marriage you learn to take a few calculated risks like that." He began to stir the paint in a bucket.

"I like to paint," said Beaver. "Give me a brush. I'll help you."

"Cut it out, Beaver," said Wally. "I already made a deal with Dad."

"Yes, Beaver," agreed Mr. Cleaver. "I'm afraid this is just a two-man job."

Beaver felt left out. "Why can't it be a three-man job?"

"Get lost," said Wally.

"Never mind, Wally," said Mr. Cleaver. "It's a two-man job because we have only two paint brushes."

Beaver had no solution for this. He sat on the back step and watched his brother and father paint the furniture. They seemed to enjoy working together in the sunny backyard and he felt more and more left out. He wasn't anybody. He wasn't a track star or a Crusader or any of the things that Wally was. He wasn't even old enough to sell hot dogs. He was just a kid brother who wasn't even good enough to help paint the patio furniture. Wally and his father wouldn't even miss him if he left.

Mrs. Cleaver came out to inspect the progress of the furniture. "How are we doing out here?" she asked.

"Coming along pretty well," answered Mr. Cleaver. "How do you like the color?"

"It looks fine," said Mrs. Cleaver. "I just hope I don't get tired of it in a year." Then she looked at Beaver. "My goodness, what is the long face for? You look as if you'd lost your best friend."

"Mom, is there some job I can do?" Beaver asked. "Wally's already got dibs on Dad."

"Well, let's see now, Beaver . . . I tell you what— why don't you empty the wastebaskets for me?"

"Will I get paid like Wally is?" Beaver wanted to know.

"Hey!" objected Wally. "Who said I'm getting paid? This is one of the jobs I'm supposed to do because I'm a member of the family."

"Yeah, but painting is fun," Beaver pointed out.

"Beaver, you empty all the wastebaskets and do a real neat job and I'll pay you a quarter," said Mrs. Cleaver. "Just empty them into the big box I left in the hall."

"O.K., Mom." Beaver accepted his mother's offer. He might as well. If he did not he would probably have to empty all the wastebaskets anyway and would not get paid for the job.

"Gee, Mom, why are you giving Beaver a whole quarter just for emptying the wastebaskets?" asked Wally. "If you start paying him that much for such an easy job at his age, by the time he gets to be my age he'll be a real wild man."

"Wally, do you think you can stop philosophizing long enough to stop dripping paint on the patio?" Mr. Cleaver rubbed at the drops of paint with an old rag.

"Sure, Dad." Wally wiped his brush carefully on the edge of the can. "I just thought emptying the waste-baskets should be one of the jobs he should do because he is a member of the family, is all."

Beaver grinned and made a face at Wally before he went into the house to start the highly paid job of emptying the wastebaskets. For once he was one up on Wally.

It was not a very interesting job, but twenty-five cents was twenty-five cents. He emptied the wastebasket from his and Wally's room and from his parents' room, but he did not find anything interesting, just an empty toothpaste box and a lot of crumpled-up paper. It was not until he emptied the wastebasket from his father's study that he discovered something worthwhile.

As Beaver turned the wastebasket upside down over the box in the downstairs hall, a stiff piece of paper with a gold seal caught his attention. It was so official looking that Beaver pulled it out of the box thinking perhaps it was something his father had thrown away by mistake. It read, "Worldwide Academy of Music. This certificate entitles Theodore Cleaver to a five-day trial of our De Luxe Stereophonic Accordion." Printed on the gold seal were the words, "Act now—absolutely free."

Boy! thought Beaver. A de luxe stereophonic accordion free for five days! But how did he go about getting it? The certificate did not say. He leaned over and rummaged through the waste paper in the box until he came upon a letter bearing the letterhead of the academy of music. Leaning against the wall he began to read, "The Worldwide Academy of Music is happy to inform you that your son, Theodore Cleaver, has been chosen as one of the few in your area to receive the advantages of our amazing free offer."

Beaver could not help being impressed. He had been chosen! That meant the Worldwide Academy of Music thought he was somebody pretty special. Hurriedly he read on. "Return the enclosed certificate and we will send you our Stereophonic Accordion for a five-day free trial. An accordion band is being formed in your locality and we are sure you want your child to participate in this cultural undertaking." Fastened to the letter with a paper clip was an envelope the size of the certificate, which said no postage was necessary.

Beaver thought it over and became more and more indignant that his father had thrown his certificate into the wastebasket. He should have been proud to have a son who was one of the few in the area to be chosen to receive the advantage of this amazing free offer. He was proud of having a son on the track team. Why couldn't he be proud of a son in an accordion band? What was the matter with him, anyway?

Beaver's indignation grew as he listened to his mother admire Wally's work on the furniture. Well, he thought, what did he have to lose? He would not even have to buy a stamp to send back the certificate. All he had to do was put it in the envelope, lick the flap and drop it into the nearest mailbox. For this he could have the de luxe stereophonic accordion to play with for five whole days.

He had never tried to play an accordion, but it looked so easy on television he had a feeling he could pick up the instrument and play it right off without even practicing. All he had to do was push and pull one end and press some keys at the other end and the music would pour out. When his father heard him he would probably want him to take part in the accordion band that was being formed and he would become famous and end up playing on television in one of those shirts made of shiny material with the baggy sleeves.

Then his father would be sorry he had thrown his son's certificate into the wastebasket. His father might even think he was good enough to help paint the patio furniture when his mother changed her mind and decided it should be a different color.

Beaver stuffed the certificate into the envelope, licked the flap and went out to drop it into the nearest mailbox. Without saying anything to his family he began to watch for the package to come. By the next Saturday when it still had not arrived he began to feel anxious. Since Wally and his father were still painting the furniture in the backyard, Beaver sat down on the front steps to wait. Sure enough, early in the afternoon an express truck stopped in front of the house and a man lifted an enormous package out of the back and carried it up the front walk.

"Does Theodore Cleaver live here?" he asked.

"Yes, sir," answered Beaver, staring in astonishment at the size of the package. "I'm him."

The man set the package on the porch and held out a receipt book to Beaver. "Just sign here, Theodore," he directed.

Beaver wrote his name on the line the man indicated, before he examined the box. He had expected a fairly large package, but this— It was so big Beaver himself could have climbed into the box. Oh well, it was probably mostly excelsior and stuff. Now he was faced with the problem of what to do with it. He jiggled the box and discovered that although it was quite heavy, it was not too heavy for him to lift. He decided the thing to do was move it upstairs to the bedroom before he unpacked it. Then he could come downstairs playing his accordion and surprise his family out in the backyard.

Beaver opened the front door and shoved his package into the house. Then he managed to get his arms around the box and to lift it from the floor. He had to feel his way along the carpet because he could not see his feet. He tripped on the steps and almost dropped his package. He had to stop several times and rest his arms before he got to the top of the stairs, where he could once more move the box by shoving it along the floor.

Beaver was busy ripping off the paper that sealed the box when Wally, smelling strongly of paint and turpentine, came into the room. "What's that?" he asked.

"My accordion," answered Beaver, hoping that he gave the impression that his package was really none of Wally's business.

"Your accordion!" exclaimed Wally.

"You heard me," said Beaver. "My accordion. Why don't you go wash and mind your own business?"

"My own business can wait," said Wally. "Where did you get an accordion?"

Beaver did not think where he got an accordion was really of any interest to Wally, but he did not want his brother to get all excited and tell their father before he had a chance to unpack the instrument and start playing it. He explained about the five-day free trial.

Wally groaned. "You little goof. This thing is probably worth a couple hundred dollars and Dad is going to blow his top when he sees it."

"It can't be worth that much," said Beaver, beginning for the first time to have some doubts about what he had done. "They wouldn't go around offering kids five days' worth of free accordion if one cost that much."

"Oh, no?" said Wally. "They figure if you take the accordion for five days you'll probably keep it."

By now Beaver had the box ripped open and was pulling out wads of paper and excelsior. "Gee . . ." Beaver sounded awed at what he saw inside—chrome, mother-of-pearl, a row of shining black and white keys. He was forced to conclude that Wally might possibly know what he was talking about. The accordion glittered splendidly and expensively. "I thought it would be one of those things more like a toy—you know like they play on television when the ladies dance around in full skirts and the men wear short pants and a feather in their hats," said Beaver.

"That's a concertina, not an accordion," said Wally, who had an irritating way of knowing a lot of things Beaver did not.

"Oh," said Beaver. "Golly, this thing is practically a piano."

"Yeah," agreed Wally. "I don't think you're even tall enough to lug around a thing like this."

"I am, too," said Beaver indignantly. "I carried the box upstairs all by myself." He grasped the exposed end of the accordion and started to pull it out of the carton. It responded with a loud drawn-out squawk.

"Wow!" exclaimed Beaver, startled.

"Cut it out, Beaver," whispered Wally. "Dad will hear you."

"I've got to squeeze it back together or it won't go in the box," Beaver whispered back. Cautiously he pushed on the accordion but in spite of his caution, the instrument gave out a loud, dismal groan.

"Sh-h!" hissed Wally.

"I couldn't help it," said Beaver.

"Boys!" Mr. Cleaver's voice came up the stairs. "What's that racket?"

Beaver swallowed. "I think it's some kind of noise."

"What kind of noise?" asked Mr. Cleaver.

"Whatever it it, I think it's going to stop now," Beaver called back.

In the meantime Wally was examining the circular that had come in the package. Now it was his turn to be awed. "Boy, Beaver, it says here this thing is worth two hundred and eighty dollars."

"Wow! Why didn't they say so in the first place?" Beaver wanted to know.

Wally continued to read. "And you don't even get to keep it five days. It came to the express office Friday. That was yesterday, and today's Saturday, and the express office is closed tomorrow. You can't send it back until after school Monday and that's the fourth day."

Beaver had an idea. "But they must have a lot of accordions at the factory. They wouldn't miss it if I didn't get it back right on time."

"Listen, Beav," Wally continued. "It says here if you don't get it back to them in five days, you've got to pay them the two hundred and eighty dollars." He shook his head as if he were disappointed in Beaver. "This is about the dumbest thing you ever did since you've been my brother. And you won't even be able to play it while you have it or Dad will start asking a lot of questions."

Regretfully Beaver had to admit Wally was right. "I better send it back Monday for sure."

"I'll say," agreed Wally. "If Dad ever finds out what you did, he'll really clobber you."

Beaver did not answer. He shoved the box into the closet, draped a couple of shirts over it and shut the door. Since he was not going to have any fun out of the accordion at all, Monday could not come soon enough to suit him. All he wanted was to get rid of the glittery, squawking thing.

Beaver spent an uneasy week end. He was afraid his mother might decide to clean out his closet and discover his accordion, and it annoyed him to have such an instrument in his possession and not be able to play it.

"What on earth is the matter with you, Beaver?"

asked Mrs. Cleaver when Mr. Cleaver was carving the Sunday roast. "I've scarcely heard a sound out of you this week end."

"Golly, Mom, I guess I just don't have much to talk about," said Beaver. After dinner he took Wally aside. "How about helping me smuggle the accordion out of the house and get it downtown to the express office after school tomorrow?" he asked.

"After you promised me you wouldn't get any more bright ideas?" said Wally with a grin.

"I just promised not to have any bright ideas about your affairs," was Beaver's explanation. "This was my own bright idea, only it turned out to be not so bright."

"It figures," said Wally good-naturedly. "O.K., I'll help you."

Monday after school Beaver, with Wally's assistance, sneaked the accordion out of the house and onto an old red wagon. Together they dragged the package downtown to the express office and boosted it up onto the counter.

"You boys shipping this box someplace?" asked the clerk.

"Yes, sir," answered Beaver. "We'd like to send it back to where it came from."

"If the box makes a noise, don't worry about it," Wally told the clerk.

"You don't have an animal in here, do you?" the man inquired.

"Oh, no sir," answered Beaver. "It's an accordion. That's not a kind of animal. It is an instrument."

"Oh, I see. Do you want it insured?" asked the clerk.

"That means if it's lost or damaged the company pays you what it's worth," Wally explained.

"Yes, I think we better have that," agreed Beaver.

If anything happened to that accordion he really would catch it. It was best to be safe.

The clerk lifted the package onto the scale. Then he did some figuring on a pad of paper. "Well, twenty-four pounds to Omaha, plus insurance. That'll be seven dollars and sixty-two cents."

Beaver was shocked. "Seven whole dollars and sixty-two cents?" he repeated, in case he had not heard correctly.

"That's right."

"How much would it cost without the insurance?" Beaver wanted to know.

The clerk did some more figuring. "Six dollars and a quarter."

Beaver turned to Wally for help.

"You better get it insured," said Wally. "How much money do you have?"

Beaver thought of his new surplus weather balloon, the movies, sodas and comic books that had taken his money lately. "Just the twenty-five cents Mom paid me for emptying the wastebaskets," he confessed, thinking that if he had not emptied the wastebaskets he would not be in this mess in the first place.

Then Beaver had an idea. "Say, Wally, how about lending me the money? Now that you aren't going to the dance you aren't going to need your hot-dog money."

"Sure I'm going to need it," said Wally. "There are lots of things I can do with money besides go to dances."

"Aw, come on, Wally, help me out," pleaded Beaver. "I'll pay you back out of my allowance."

"You boys just settle this between you," said the man behind the counter, and went about his business.

"That will take a long time," Wally pointed out.

"I'll ask Mom to let me empty the wastebaskets some more. I'll ask her to pay me to do all kinds of jobs. Come on, Wally. We don't want to have to haul the accordion home again. Dad might catch us and start asking a lot of questions." Beaver waited hopefully for his brother's answer.

Wally realized that by now he was involved in Beaver's problem and he might have to answer some of his father's questions himself. "Well, O.K., but remember, you have to pay me back every cent." He pulled his wallet out of his hip pocket.

Beaver watched anxiously as Wally counted out seven dollars and sixty-two cents and handed it to the man behind the counter. The man lifted the box containing the accordion and added it to the pile of packages on the floor. Beaver felt suddenly free. That chrome and mother-of-pearl accordion was out of his hands forever. He never wanted to see an accordion again. Beaver promised himself that he would never even watch an accordion player on television.

As soon as the brothers left the express office Beaver felt so good he leapfrogged over a fire hydrant. Then, pulling the empty wagon behind him, he walked along beside Wally. "Gee, thanks a lot, Wally," he said. "You sure saved my life."

Wally did not care about being thanked. "That's O.K. I know how Dad is."

Beaver let the wagon bump down a curb, pulled it across the street and tugged it up over the next curb. "You know, Wally, I have been pretty good lately about not getting mixed up in your affairs," he said.

"Yeah," agreed Wally. "This time you just got me mixed up in your affairs."

"I know," admitted Beaver, but being eager for praise

from his older brother, he pressed his point. "But I haven't caused you any *trouble* like I did when I brought Nick home."

Wally grinned. "Just keep up the good work, Beav," he said. "Just keep up the good work."

WALLY'S GLAMOUR GIRL

Wally was not the only member of the family to receive letters. One Saturday morning the Cleavers were eating a leisurely breakfast when the mail was delivered. Among the usual advertisements and bills was a letter for Mrs. Cleaver, which she read while she sipped her coffee.

"It's from Margaret Benson. You know, Kitty Benson's mother," she remarked as she read.

"Wally knows," said Beaver. "He writes to Kitty all the time."

"Aw, keep quiet," said Wally, looking embarrassed.

"Margaret and Kitty are coming back to Mayfield for a visit next week end. They're going to stay with the Millers," continued Mrs. Cleaver. "And guess what, Wally?"

"Uh ... what?"

"Kitty's invited you to the dance at the Mayfield Country Club," said Mrs. Cleaver.

Wally gulped, choked and quickly drank some milk.

At this Beaver became interested in the conversation. "Hey, Wally, isn't that the dance you were going to take Mary Ellen Rogers to and buy her an orchid and a lot of expensive food only you changed your mind?"

"Yeah," was all Wally had to say.

"What's the matter, son?" asked Mr. Cleaver. "You look a little strange."

"No, I don't, Dad," said Wally. "I don't have to take Kitty to the dance even if she asked me. All I have to do is say no, thank you."

Mrs. Cleaver laid the letter beside her plate. "Why Wally Cleaver, you have to go, you do too. You said yourself you didn't have a date. Margaret Benson says you wrote to Kitty all about the big dance at the country club, two weeks from tonight, and I'm sure she thought you were too shy to come right out and ask Kitty. She probably thought you were hinting for an invitation. Of course you have to accept. Margaret Benson is an old friend of mine."

"I'm not too shy to ask her, for Pete's sake," said Wally. "I just . . . have basketball practice, is all."

"Wally . . . basketball season is over, remember?" Mr. Cleaver's voice held a warning note.

"O.K., O.K., I just don't want to ask her, is all," confessed Wally.

"You don't have to ask her," Mr. Cleaver pointed out. "She has already asked you."

"And you like her a lot," said Beaver. "You write to her all the time and she writes back on pink paper."

"I wish my whole family would keep out of my business," said Wally. "It's getting so a fellow can't lift his little finger without his whole family jumping on him."

"We won't jump on you," said Mr. Cleaver amiably. "You just sit down and write Kitty a nice note accepting her invitation and we won't jump on you at all. And then the night of the dance you put on your blue suit and I'll drive you and Kitty to the country club and bring you home at twelve and you'll enjoy every minute of it—or else."

Wally threw down his napkin. "May I please be excused?"

"Now what do you suppose is the matter with him?" wondered Mrs. Cleaver when Wally had left the room.

Beaver did not know what was the matter with Wally but he was certainly interested in finding out. He finished his breakfast as quickly as he could without having his mother tell him not to eat so fast, and joined his brother in their room. "You really wanted to get away from Mom and Dad so they wouldn't keep telling you to go out with that Kitty girl, didn't you?" he asked.

"Look, Beaver," said Wally, "it's bad enough having a kid brother. You don't have to go and make it worse by being right all the time."

"What's wrong with you going out with Kitty Benson—outside of her being a girl?" asked Beaver.

"You wouldn't understand," muttered Wally.

This hurt Beaver's feelings. No boy likes to have his older brother tell him he wouldn't understand. "No, I don't understand," said Beaver crossly. "You've been writing to her all the time, so you must like her."

"Aw . . . I like her all right, I guess. Except that . . ." Wally apparently did not know how to finish what he had started to say. "Look, it's like this. Last summer when I was away at camp a lot of the boys were getting letters from girls and reading them out loud and . . . well, that made them real big shots. I guess I wanted to be a big shot, too."

"You mean you started writing to Kitty so she'd write back to you?" Now Beaver was beginning to understand why Wally had been writing letters to Kitty in the first place.

Wally opened the drawer of his desk and took his pen and notepaper. Then he sat staring into space.

"You writing to Kitty now?" asked Beaver.

"Yeah."

"What are you going to tell her?" Beaver wanted to know.

"Well, first I'll tell her I'll be happy to go to the dance with her," said Wally.

Beaver objected to this. "But you aren't happy to go with her. How come you're telling her you are?"

"Because it's good manners to say you're happy to go with someone even though you'd rather be dead. And besides, Dad may want to read the letter to make sure I am polite," explained Wally. "Now beat it, will you? I've got to give this letter an awful lot of thought."

This sounded very mysterious to Beaver, who decided it was best to leave the room since Wally quite plainly did not want him around. He was puzzled, though. He could not understand why Wally could write so many letters to a girl and then not be willing to take her to a dance.

Beaver gave Wally plenty of time to finish the letter before he returned to the room, but when he opened the door he found Wally still sitting at his desk. His hair was rumpled, there was a smudge of ink on his cheek and the wastebasket was filled with crumpled paper. He looked up from his work to glare at Beaver.

"Don't look at me," said Beaver. "I didn't do anything." He opened the closet to take out his jacket.

"Oh no?"

Wally sounded so bitter that Beaver turned around. Wally was still glaring at him.

"You've done just about everything," said Wally.

"If you hadn't done all the things you did I wouldn't be in this mess."

"What things?" Beaver could not imagine what Wally was talking about.

"Things like bringing home Nick the horse instead of the ten dollars I earned, and losing Chuckie in the shoe department so his mother didn't pay me and borrowing practically all of my money to send back an accordion you shouldn't have had in the first place." Wally's anger seemed to be mounting. "Every time I do something, my kid brother has to come along and mess everything up."

Beaver backed toward the door. "Gee, Wally, I told you I wasn't going to mess up your affairs any more and I haven't. That accordion business wasn't your affair."

"O.K., so I helped you out," said Wally bitterly, "and now I am in the worst mess of all. Me and my good deeds!"

"I paid you back fifty cents when I got my allowance," Beaver reminded Wally.

"Fifty cents! A lot of good that will do with a girl like Kitty." Wally crumpled another sheet of paper and tossed it into the wastebasket. "A girl like Kitty— Well, she needs at least two orchids, and now I can't afford even one."

"Two orchids!" This to Beaver was an outlandish waste of perfectly good money. The price of two orchids would probably buy several surplus weather balloons. If Wally was so anxious to give a girl flowers why couldn't he go out in the yard and pick a couple of snapdragons or something, instead of getting all worked up and taking it out on Beaver? "She didn't go around wearing two orchids when she lived in Mayfield, did she?" he asked. "I'll bet she didn't wear any orchids. She was just a plain old girl."

Wally seemed less angry. "Things are different now," he said moodily. He doodled on his desk blotter a while before he said, "I laid it on real thick in those letters I wrote her from camp so she'd think I was really something and would write me letters that would make me look like a . . . you know . . . a swinger."

Beaver came back into the room and sat down on the bed. This was getting interesting. "Boy, Wally, what kind of stuff did she write you?" And here Beaver had thought he was the only one in the family who ever got into trouble by exaggerating!

Wally opened the drawer of his desk and pulled out a bundle of letters. He opened one and read, "Dearest Wally—"

Beaver interrupted. "How come she calls you mushy junk like 'dearest'?"

"On account of I called her 'honey' and said I liked her, in the letter before. I did that so she would write me some good stuff I could read to the fellows at camp," explained Wally.

"Read some more, Wally." Beaver was eager to hear more.

Wally continued. " 'I stayed awake all last night thinking about your last letter. It's wonderful to think that such a darling, popular boy—with his own car and tuxedo and everything—really cares about little old me.' "

"Your own car and tuxedo?" Where did this Kitty get such ideas, Beaver wondered.

"That's what I mean," said Wally miserably. "Kitty really has a car of her own on account of her Pop's got a whole lot of money. So I had to write her I had a car so she wouldn't think I was a creep."

"Wow!" exclaimed Beaver, who certainly had never exaggerated himself into a car and a tuxedo.

"And she has two fur coats and a whole bunch of evening gowns," continued Wally. "And here's her picture." He tossed a wrinkled, smudged snapshot to Beaver, who was sitting on his bed.

Beaver studied the picture. It was a girl in an evening gown, all right, but he could not tell much about her face. "I don't know. She doesn't look like so much to me."

"Well, that's because I had it in my pocket at camp," Wally explained. "Some guy pushed me in the lake and her face dissolved."

Beaver shook his head. "Boy, Wally, I thought when you grew up you were supposed to get smarter."

"I guess I got dumber instead," said Wally. "The whole thing just got away from me. I wrote her about how Dad was president of the bank and about how I went to big society dances all the time."

Beaver shook his head. It was too bad about Wally. He used to be such a smart fellow . . . good grades . . . star of the track team . . . and now look at him, growing dumber every day.

Wally picked up another letter from the pink pile. "Here's the last letter she wrote me. I don't know if I should tell you about it or not."

"Come on, Wally." Beaver did not want to miss a thing. "The only kind of letters I ever get are asking me to subscribe to magazines or go to birthday parties."

Wally hesitated. "Well . . . it ends, 'Yours forever, Kitty.' "

"Wow!" Beaver could see that Wally was really stuck

with this Kitty. "Yours forever" sounded pretty permanent.

Wally shoved all the pink letters back into his drawer and began to write.

Beaver watched Wally's pen moving across the paper until he could contain his curiosity no longer. "What are you writing, Wally?" he asked.

Wally laid down his pen. "Well, first I said 'Dear Miss Benson' . . . That's to cancel out all that mushy stuff I've been writing her."

"Yeah." Beaver agreed this was a sound idea.

Wally read, " 'I'll be happy to go to the dance with you even in spite of the accident and everything.' "

Wally scowled at Beaver and read on. " 'I don't know had any accident."

Wally scowled at Beaver and read on. "I don't know if you heard, but I went to a fancy party last week and a car smashed my car in the parking lot.' "

"Boy!" exclaimed Beaver. Wally's imagination was really wild. "Go on."

" 'On account of it is being fixed, I thought it would be fun if my Dad drove us to the dance. I asked my father and he laughed and said it isn't everybody that can have a bank president for a chauffeur.' "

"That takes care of the car, but what about the tuxedo?" Beaver asked.

Here Wally hesitated. "Well . . . I thought I could tell her Mom loaned it to somebody who spilled something on it. What do you think, Beaver?"

"What do you think, Wally?" Beaver countered.

For answer, Wally crumpled the whole letter and threw it into the wastebasket. Then he took another sheet of paper and picked up his pen. "I'm just going to write her a regular letter not saying I'm happy to take her to the dance, and then I hope I croak before Saturday."

This seemed to Beaver like a sensible thing to do and he was about to say so, when Wally was suddenly angry again. "So you see, Beav, if it weren't for you I would be in only half this mess. If you hadn't messed up my financial affairs I could have afforded one orchid. And maybe even a taxi. The way it is now Kitty is going to have everybody at that country-club dance laughing at me and practically everybody in Mayfield is going to be there."

Beaver knew it was no use answering Wally. He now felt genuinely sorry for his brother even though he felt the whole thing was Wally's fault for having anything to do with girls in the first place. Beaver resolved to have nothing to do with girls when he reached high school. That was the best way he knew of to stay out of trouble.

Beaver felt so sorry for Wally that he went downstairs and asked his mother if he could empty the wastebaskets again to earn another twenty-five cents. His mother told him that emptying the wastebaskets was something he should do because he was part of the family and that she had only paid him the first time because he had felt left out when Wally and his father were painting the patio furniture. Then she suggested that he empty the wastebaskets right now. Beaver did as he was told but he was careful not to look at anything in any of the baskets. He did not want to get mixed up with any more certificates that offered a five-day free trial of anything.

After that Beaver stayed away from Wally as much as he could. There was nothing he could do to help and he did not like to see Wally looking so unhappy.

One day at dinner Mrs. Cleaver, noticing that Wally was eating in silence, remarked, "I don't know, Ward. It seems to me things were different when I was a girl. When there was a country-club dance to look forward to all the young people were happy about it. They didn't go around with long faces."

"Uh . . . that reminds me," said Wally. "Dad, I was wondering if maybe you could lend me a couple of dollars until after the dance. I'll have some extra expenses."

"Why certainly, Wally. I know how it is." Mr. Cleaver reached into his pocket, pulled out his wallet and handed Wally two one-dollar bills.

"Thanks, Dad." Wally managed to smile for the first time since Kitty's mother's letter had arrived. "Now I can take Kitty to the dance in a taxi and you won't have to drive us."

"Now wait a minute, Wally," said Mr. Cleaver. "There is no point in your wasting money on taxis when I can drive you to the dance. And while we are on the subject of money, what did you do with the ten dollars you earned selling hot dogs at the lake?"

Beaver held his breath.

Wally shrugged. "It just got away from me, I guess."

"Wally, I think it's time you learned to take better care of your money," said Mr. Cleaver. "And you can start by letting me drive you to the dance."

Wally started to protest. "Gee, Dad—" Then he apparently decided it would be useless to argue, because he did not finish whatever it was he had started to say. It was the quietest meal the Cleavers had eaten since the time Wally threw a baseball through the windshield of his father's car.

Beaver felt worse and worse. Poor Wally who had always been so good to his kid brother . . . had helped him learn to play ball . . . had helped him smuggle the accordion out of the house and paid the express charges and never said a word about it to his father . . . Beaver did not know what he would do without Wally.

Beaver began to dread Saturday night for his brother's sake. On Saturday afternoon before the dance he could not stand staying home watching Wally be miserable, so he and Whitey walked over to State Street, which had just been made a one-way street. They spent an interesting afternoon watching people getting tickets for driving the wrong way on the one-way street.

Wally was no more cheerful when Beaver returned. He did mention that Eddie Haskell had suggested that he eat about a quart of chocolate syrup and then drink a whole bottle of vinegar. If he did that he wouldn't be able to go to a dance for a week.

"You're kidding, Wally," said Beaver, when he heard of this scheme of Eddie's. It was easy enough for Eddie to suggest something like this. He was not planning to drink the mixture himself.

"Yeah, I guess I'm kidding," said Wally gloomily, as he looked at his watch. "Now it's only four hours till doomsday."

At dinner Beaver said, "Say Dad, when you take Wally to pick up Kitty, can I go along?"

"No, you can't," said Wally fiercely. "It's bad enough having to have Dad drive me without a kid brother tagging along."

"Don't get excited, Wally," said Beaver. "I was only asking."

"Don't be so grouchy, Wally," said his mother. "You're going to a dance tonight to have a good time. Remember?"

"Yeah, I know."

The despair in Wally's voice made Beaver feel worse than ever. Poor old Wally. He felt almost as miserable as Wally while Wally took a shower, put on his good blue suit and rubbed the lilac-smelling stuff on his hair. He watched Wally take the corsage he had bought that afternoon out of the refrigerator. It was two inexpensive gardenias instead of two expensive orchids.

"Anyway, they smell pretty," said Beaver, hoping somehow to console his brother.

"Yeah," was all Wally said.

The evening seemed lonely with Wally away dancing at the country club. Beaver could not get interested in television. He even took a bath without his mother's reminding him. He pictured Kitty in a beautiful evening gown trimmed with little glittery things and wearing a fur coat, laughing at Wally in his blue suit. She would probably tell everybody how Wally had written her his father was president of the bank, and everybody at the dance would laugh at Wally. And if Mary Ellen Rogers had laughed at Wally in his hot-dog suit she would really laugh at him now. And Eddie Haskell—he would never forget something like this.

When Beaver went to bed it took him a long time to go to sleep. He lay in bed thinking about the terrible evening Wally was having and how he was at least partly to blame for it. He would make it up to Wally somehow. It seemed to him that he had not really been asleep at all when he was aware of a crack of light around the bathroom door. Then he heard someone humming. Beaver raised himself up on his elbow.

"Wally?" he whispered.

The bathroom door opened a crack and Wally stuck his head out. "You want something, Beaver?" he asked.

"Did they laugh at you much?" Beaver wanted to know.

Wally came out and sat down on the foot of Beaver's bed. He was actually smiling. "Heck, no. Kitty was wearing a pink dress like any other girl and she was scared to go with me because she had written a lot of silly stuff because she thought I was rich and glamorous. Her letters were just as phony as mine. And that picture she sent wasn't even her. It was her older sister."

"Gee . . ." Beaver needed a moment to take all this in.

"And you know what?" Wally asked and did not wait for an answer. "She likes gardenias and she doesn't even like orchids because they don't have a pretty smell."

"Golly . . ."

"And you know something else?" Wally went on. "Mary Ellen Rogers was there with Eddie Haskell and we traded dances and she said she was sorry she laughed at me in my hot-dog suit. She said she really admired me for taking the job when I didn't get to be a lifeguard. And she said she didn't even tell Eddie she would go to the dance with him until she heard I was taking Kitty, because she hoped I would ask her."

"Well . . ." This was a surprise. Beaver felt he had wasted the whole evening worrying about Wally when he could have been watching television. "Say, Wally, you aren't still mad at me about the accordion, are you?" he asked.

"Aw, I guess not," said Wally agreeably. "All kids get into messes sometimes."

Beaver did not much care about having Wally call him a kid but he was glad his brother was no longer angry with him. He was also glad to know that after all his worry Wally had had a good time. It was puzzling to Beaver, who could not help thinking that Wally would do better to stick to track and basketball instead of wasting his time thinking about girls so much. Girls weren't worth all the worry.

"You know something, Wally?" he said, as Wally began to undress. "You're never going to catch me having girl troubles. No, sir! I'm never going to go near a girl."

Wally laughed. "You want to bet?" he asked, and turned out the light.

BEAVER AND VIOLET

Even though Wally's experience with Kitty and Mary Ellen finally had a happy ending, Beaver kept his vow to stay as far from girls as he could. You would never catch him worrying and fretting about girls and wasting money on them. Not Beaver Cleaver. Never very friendly with Judy Hensler and Violet Rutherford, he was now careful to avoid them altogether, even though to be perfectly honest about it, Judy and Violet did not appear to be eager for his company either. Nevertheless, it gave Beaver a sort of satisfaction to turn and go the other way when he saw them coming down the hall. If he was going to avoid girls all his life, now was the time to start.

And so when Mrs. Cleaver announced that the Cleavers and the Rutherfords were going on a picnic together to Friend's Lake, Beaver was not at all pleased. Violet Rutherford would be there and he did not look forward to listening to her giggle all day. He would much rather stay home and play with Whitey Whitney. It was unfortunate that his father and Violet's father worked in the same office.

Then he discovered that Wally did not want to go on the picnic either, but his reason was the opposite of Beaver's. Beaver did not want to go because he wanted to stay away from a girl—Violet Rutherford. Wally did not want to go because he wanted to be near a girl—

Mary Ellen Rogers. The two boys stood on the front steps surrounded by thermos bottles, potato chips, and cartons containing cake and potato salad and agreed that they did not want to have anything to do with this picnic.

"Aw, Mom, do I have to go?" asked Wally as he helped carry picnic equipment out to the front steps.

"Why can't Wally go and I stay home?" asked Beaver.

"You both have to go," said Mrs. Cleaver, "and that is that."

"Cheer up, boys," said Mr. Cleaver as he set the thermos jug beside the box of picnic food. "You're going on a picnic and picnics are fun. Remember?"

Beaver made a face. "Not with old Violet Rutherford along."

"Why, Beaver, she's a friend of yours," said Mrs. Cleaver, adding four sweaters to the pile on the steps. "She's in your class."

"Sure she's in my class, but she's not a friend of mine," said Beaver. "She's a girl."

"It might not be so bad, Beav," said Wally. "If she hangs around too much, you can throw bugs on her or something."

"Yeah," agreed Beaver, "and if I find a dead fish I could chase her with it."

"Aw, gee, Mom, you know how it's going to be. We'll have to listen to Mr. Rutherford's corny old jokes all afternoon."

"Yeah," agreed Beaver. "Mr. Rutherford is the only one who ever laughs at his jokes."

Mr. Cleaver laughed. "How do you know one of his jokes might not turn out to be funny someday?"

"I'll keep hoping," said Wally, "but I've never heard a good one yet."

"Me neither," said Beaver.

Then the Rutherford car pulled up in front of the Cleaver house and Violet and her parents climbed out. Beaver stared without expression at his classmate. It was bad enough having to see her five days a week without seeing her on Saturday, too.

"Beaver," whispered his mother as the two families greeted one another, "say hello to Violet."

"Hello, Violet," said Beaver.

"Hello, Beaver," answered Violet. At least she did not giggle.

Mr. Rutherford, a tall, bald-headed, serious-looking man who wore glasses, opened the trunk of the car. "I like to stow things away all shipshape and Bristol fashion," he remarked.

"Just like a boat, eh, Fred?" said Mr. Cleaver with a grin.

"Of course, Ward—that's the expression. Bristol's a seafaring port in England," answered Mr. Rutherford, as if they did not know.

"It's a beautiful day for a picnic," remarked Mrs. Cleaver as she carried the thermos jug out to the car.

"Fred arranged it that way," said Mrs. Rutherford, and laughed.

Beaver and Wally exchanged a glance. Now Mrs. Rutherford was making corny jokes, too.

Mr. Rutherford took the thermos jug from Mrs. Cleaver. "Better let me stow that, June. We don't want anything tipping over in a high sea." He laughed heartily at his own joke. Beaver and Wally did not.

When the last sweater was packed away, Mr. Rutherford slammed the trunk of the car.

"Well, Fred, shall we heave anchor and get this windjammer on the road?" asked Mr. Cleaver jovially.

Beaver and Wally exchanged a disgusted look. Now their own father was doing it. This picnic was getting worse and worse and they had not even started.

"June, you sit in the back by the window," said Mr. Rutherford, who was inclined to be bossy. "Ward, you're in the middle and Gwen, you're next." He closed the rear door when everyone was seated to his satisfaction. Then he slid into the driver's seat. "Now let the skipper get here at the wheel . . . Wally, you're next. Now Beaver."

"But Daddy, where do I sit?" asked Violet when Beaver was seated.

"Violet, you just squeeze in beside Beaver," directed her father. "There's plenty of width in these new cars for two big people and two little people in the front seat."

That's what you think, thought Beaver, smarting at being referred to as "little people," as Violet squeezed in beside him and slammed the door. He moved as close to Wally as he could, but Violet was still pressed against him. Squashed against old Violet Rutherford all the way to Friend's Lake! How terrible was this picnic going to get, anyway?

He glanced at Violet out of the corner of his eye, but she was staring straight ahead. Well, she'd better. One giggle out of her and he would . . . well, he would do something drastic. He didn't know what. Things soon got worse. The first thing that happened was passing Whitey and Gilbert playing ball on the sidewalk. Beaver did not see why they couldn't keep their eyes on the ball, but no, they both had to look at the Ruther-

ford's car and see him all squashed against Violet
Rutherford.

"Hey, look at old Beaver!" Whitey announced to the
world.

"Woo-woo!" yelled Gilbert.

"Hey, Beaver, you're doing all right!" shouted
Whitey.

Beaver slid as far down on the seat as he could and
Violet continued to stare straight ahead all the way to
Friend's Lake.

At the picnic grounds Beaver began to feel hopeful
that things might take a turn for the better. Violet
helped the two mothers with the food and he and
Wally had no trouble escaping. They rented two fishing
rods, bought some worms and settled down to fish at
the edge of the lake some distance away from Violet.
The sun was warm, the sky was blue and Beaver forgot
about Violet and Mr. Rutherford's unfunny jokes. He
and Wally fished in companionable silence. This was
the life, thought Beaver. No girls around. No fish either,
but he did not care.

That is, Beaver forgot about Violet until she suddenly walked up behind him.

"Hi, Beaver," she said. "What are you doing?"

Beaver started. It had all been so peaceful until this
moment. "We're fishing," he said impatiently. "What
did you think we're doing?"

"What are you fishing for?" persisted Violet.

"We're fishing for fish," answered Beaver, even more
impatiently.

"That's what I thought," said Violet. "They want
you."

"Who wants us?" asked Wally.

"Your folks and my folks," answered Violet.

"Oh, all right." Wally scowled. There was no escaping Violet or her father.

With great reluctance the boys gathered up their tackle and followed Violet back to the picnic table, where the two sets of parents were taking snapshots. "Oh, great," muttered Wally. "Now we've got to smile and look at the birdie."

"I sure don't feel like smiling," said Beaver. "I feel like fishing or eating."

"Well, boys, where are the fish?" asked Mr. Cleaver.

"I guess they're still in the lake," answered Wally.

"Let's have some pictures of the younger generation," said Mr. Rutherford jovially. "Shall we start off with you and Violet, Beaver?"

Beaver did not want his picture taken with Violet, but he did not dare say so right out loud. "Do I have to, Mom?" he whispered.

"Now, Beaver, don't make a fuss," his mother whispered back. "It won't hurt a bit."

Beaver gave his mother a pleading look but she motioned him toward Violet. Beaver dragged his feet as he walked toward the girl. Catching a glimpse of Wally trying not to laugh did not help any. He stopped about a yard away from Violet and faced the camera.

Mr. Rutherford, who was looking into the camera, motioned to Beaver. "Get a little closer together. I can't get you both in the finder."

Beaver took a small step toward Violet, who took a large step toward him. Mr. Rutherford had better not tell him to smile. He *couldn't* smile, not when he was this close to old Violet.

"Come on, Beaver, look like you enjoy it," directed Mr. Rutherford. "Violet, put your arm around him."

Beaver tried to pull away but Violet put her arm

around him anyway and hung on. He was glad Whitey wasn't around to see *this*. He looked toward his mother and father, hoping that somehow they would help him out, but they only smiled at him and appeared to be amused at the whole thing. Beaver felt that he would just as soon face a firing squad as Mr. Rutherford and that camera.

"Don't they look sweet together?" murmured Mrs. Rutherford.

Beaver gritted his teeth.

"Now . . . all set?" asked Mr. Rutherford. "Give him a big kiss, Violet."

Beaver stood frozen with surprise while Violet planted a kiss on his cheek at the exact moment the camera clicked. Then he broke away from her and ran. He ran across the picnic grounds and past the beach crowded with swimmers and sun bathers. He ran to a clump of bushes by the woodsy edge of the lake and hid. He was mad at his family for not rescuing him, he was mad at Mr. Rutherford for taking the picture and he was especially mad at Violet for kissing him. She did not have to go and mind her father so promptly, did she? She could have stalled until after he had taken the picture.

Beaver stayed hidden and began to get hungry. He pictured the others eating all that good potato salad and chocolate cake while he was a starving refugee from Violet and her father. He felt pretty sorry for himself until Wally found him and brought him some sandwiches and cake. This made Beaver feel better—toward Wally at least. When it was time to go home his father came and dragged him out of the bushes. Beaver did not speak to Violet all the way home. She did not speak to him, either. She knew she did not dare.

The next week at school Beaver would not even look at Violet. He tried to pretend she was not in the classroom. He was not going to go around talking to a girl who had kissed him in front of a camera. As for his family, he scowled so ferociously every time they tried to tease him about Violet that they stopped teasing him and appeared to forget the whole incident. Even Wally, who probably wished he had been in front of the camera with Mary Ellen Rogers kissing him, let the matter drop.

Then one day Beaver brought Whitey Whitney home with him from school. The boys went into Mr. Cleaver's study to get some pencils and when Beaver pulled open the drawer of his father's desk, he gasped at what he saw inside. There was a copy of his father's office magazine, *The Weekly Memo*. On the cover was the picture of Violet kissing him.

It was not snapshot size, either. It had been enlarged so that it filled up the whole cover. There was Beaver with his eyes wide with surprise and Violet with her eyes closed and her puckered-up lips planted on Beaver's cheek. You could even see the freckles on her nose. Beaver started to slam the drawer shut but he was too late. Whitey had already seen the picture.

"Boy!" exclaimed Whitey, snatching the magazine out of the drawer.

"You give me that!" ordered Beaver and grabbed the magazine away from Whitey.

"Aw, come on, Beaver," said Whitey. "Let me see it. I won't tell."

Beaver could not help being fascinated by the picture. He and Whitey read the caption underneath. "A Future Merger?" it read.

"What were you and Violet doing that for?" asked Whitey.

"Because her father ordered us to, that's why," answered Beaver. "You don't think I want old Violet Rutherford kissing me, do you?"

Whitey laughed. "Wait till the kids at school find out about this!"

"How are they going to find out?" demanded Beaver. "*I* won't tell them!"

"O.K., O.K.," said Whitey. "I'm no Indian promiser." He looked at the picture again. "You know what this means? It means Violet Rutherford is in love with you!"

Beaver thought this pretty far-fetched. "Aw, go on, Whitey. She is not."

"Sure she is," Whitey assured him. "All the people in the movies who kiss each other are in love."

Beaver considered. Maybe Whitey was right. Maybe that was why Violet went ahead and kissed him so promptly when her father told her to. She was in love with him like Wally was in love with Mary Ellen Rogers. "I never had a girl in love with me before," he said dubiously. "What should I do?"

"Gee, I don't know." Whitey sounded sympathetic. "I never had a girl in love with me either. But you know something? Getting your picture in here and everything —you're kind of famous."

"Aw, who wants to be famous for kissing?" Beaver wanted to know. "If I'm going to be famous, I want to be famous for fighting or rescuing people or something like that. Kissing—ugh!"

Just then Wally stuck his head in the door of the study. "Hey, Beav, you're wanted on the telephone. It's Violet Rutherford."

Beaver and Whitey looked at one another and Beaver was forced to conclude that Whitey was right. Violet was not only in love with him, she was calling him up to tell him so. "Tell her I'm not at home, Wally. Tell her I'm not going to be home for the rest of my life!"

"O.K., she's your girl friend, not mine," said Wally.

"She is not my girl friend," contradicted Beaver.

"But I think that as long as her dad and our dad work in the same office, I'll just tell her you aren't home," Wally said and disappeared.

"Boy, Beaver, now she's chasing you," said Whitey. "You're going to have a hard time keeping away from her when you're in the same room at school."

This was exactly what Beaver was thinking.

The next day at school he felt as if Violet were everywhere. When Richard walked up behind him and said, "Hi," Beaver jumped. "Oh!" he said, startled.

"What's the matter, Beav?" asked Richard.

"Nothing," answered Beaver. "I thought you were a girl."

"Cut it out, will you?" said Richard. "I got a haircut yesterday."

"I thought you were Violet Rutherford," Beaver admitted.

"Why should you be scared of her?" asked Richard. "She's just a girl."

"I'm not scared of her," said Beaver. "I just don't want to see her, is all."

"Well, in case you're interested," said Richard, looking down the hall, "here she comes now."

Beaver felt trapped. "Do me a favor, Richard," he begged. "Tell her you haven't seen me for a long time."

He ducked into a classroom, where he stood near the door so he could listen.

Sure enough, Violet said, "Richard, have you seen Beaver Cleaver?"

"No," answered Richard. "Beaver told me to tell you I haven't seen him in a long time."

That was close, thought Beaver, as he peeked out and saw Violet walking on down the hall. She was in love with him, all right, if she went around asking about him that way. She was probably heartbroken because she hadn't found him.

Later that day Whitey stopped Beaver by the drinking fountain and asked, "Hey, did Violet catch you yet?"

"Uh-uh . . . and she's not going to," answered Beaver. "That's why I didn't go out to the playground."

"I saw her looking at you in class," said Whitey.

"Was it a love look?" asked Beaver.

"No, it was kind of a dumb look," said Whitey.

"I think that's the same thing," said Beaver.

"Yeah . . . oh-oh, here she comes now," said Whitey.

"Quick, stand in front of me." Beaver turned and bent over the drinking fountain and Whitey stepped in front of him.

"Hi, Whitey," said Violet.

"Hi, Violet."

"Have you seen Beaver?" asked Violet.

"Beaver? I think I saw him going the other way."

"Oh." Violet sounded disappointed.

When he was sure it was safe, Beaver straightened up.

"Boy, Beaver," said Whitey, "having a girl in love with you is a lot rougher than I thought it was."

"Yeah," agreed Beaver. "She'll probably get bloodhounds out after me next. You know what I'm going to

do? I'm going to stay in class after school till everyone's
gone home."

True to his word, Beaver did stay in the classroom
until he saw Violet leave. He waited a little longer until
everyone had gone home, just to make sure, and was just
starting toward the door when Violet unexpectedly returned. Beaver looked wildly around but everyone had
gone. He and Violet were alone and she was blocking
the only exit to the room. He was trapped. He watched
her come toward him and wondered desperately if she
were going to try to kiss him again and what he should
do if she did try. It would not do to hit a girl.

"Hello, Beaver," said Violet, "I've been looking for
you all day."

"Yeah, well, I've got to go home and help my
mother," said Beaver, looking over Violet's shoulder at
the door and wondering if he dared make a run for it
and if Violet would try to tackle him if he did.

"I saw our picture on the magazine," said Violet.

"What about it?" Beaver asked crossly.

"Well, I want to tell you something," said Violet.

"You better not," said Beaver, who was in no mood
to listen to any mushy talk. "I don't want to hear it."

"I'm going to tell you anyway," said Violet. "I only
kissed you because my father told me to and I knew I
would catch it when I got home if I didn't do what he
said. I don't like you at all."

This was exactly the opposite of what Beaver had
expected to hear. "No fooling?" he asked, wanting to
be reassured that Violet really meant what she said.

"Of course I'm not fooling." Violet sounded every
bit as cross as Beaver had. "You're like all boys. You're
dirty and messy and you do mean things."

Suddenly Beaver grinned. "Gee, I was hoping you didn't like me, but I was afraid to ask you."

"No, I don't like you," snapped Violet. "Not one little bit. I'd rather kiss a dead lizard than kiss you again."

This was the nicest thing anyone had said to Beaver for a long time. "Hey, that's neat, Violet, because I don't like you either."

"Don't you dare go showing that picture to anybody." Violet sounded almost ferocious.

"Don't worry. I already burned it and I spit on the ashes." This was not strictly true. Beaver had hidden the picture under his mattress where nobody would see it, but as soon as he went home he would burn it in the incinerator and he really would spit on the ashes.

This seemed to cheer Violet. "I'm glad you feel that way," she said, sounding almost pleasant, "because if you didn't I was going to ask my father to let me change schools." With a toss of her hair she turned and started toward the door.

"You know something, Violet?" said Beaver.

"What?" she asked, pausing but not turning around.

"You're not so bad for a girl."

Violet glanced over her shoulder and smiled. "You're not so bad for a boy, either."

Beaver smiled, too. It was pretty neat when a girl he thought liked him turned out not to like him. It made him feel good to have her think he was dirty and mean and messy. He felt like swaggering just to show how dirty and mean and messy he was. "Uh . . . Violet . . . what a minute, will you?"

"What for?" asked Violet, but she waited.

Beaver decided she really wasn't so bad, standing

there with her nose in the air and not giggling. For a girl she was even pretty nice, because she thought he was dirty and mean and messy. "Uh . . . since we're both leaving at the same time suppose I sort of . . . walk with you."

"O.K.," agreed Violet, and together they walked out of the building.

Then Violet walked along one edge of the sidewalk and Beaver, kicking the grass, walked along the other. They could not find anything to say to one another.

Beaver wondered if this was the way Wally had felt about Mary Ellen Rogers. He tried to picture himself wanting to give Violet an orchid. He could not. He could not even picture himself wanting to give her a petunia. Still, for a girl she wasn't too awful. Beaver felt confused about the whole thing.

Then Beaver tried to picture himself going off to camp like Wally and wondered if Violet would write to him. Letters about . . . stuff. Letters like Wally got from Kitty Benson. He could picture the going-to-camp part but he wasn't so sure about the letters.

"Uh . . . Violet," began Beaver, who felt that as long as he was walking home with Violet he had to find something to say. "Supposing I went off to camp and wrote you a letter. Would you write back?"

"Oh, Beaver! I would love to," said Violet enthusiastically. "I've always wanted a pen pal. When are you going to camp?"

"I don't know," said Beaver vaguely. "Someday, I guess." It was nice to know that a girl would write to him if he wrote to her, since he knew that was what fellows Wally's age did when they went to camp. "I'll write you when I get there."

And with that Beaver resolved to go home, take the picture of Violet kissing him out from under the mattress and burn it in the incinerator. But he wouldn't really spit on the ashes.